Kat McGee and

"Please give yourself a treat and read this book…I'm SO GLAD that I did."
—*I Love to Read and Review Books*

"The seminal work on Mrs. Claus."
—Santa Claus

Praise for
Kat McGee and The Halloween Costume Caper

"A wild cross between Magic Tree House and The Nightmare Before Christmas. Kat McGee is madcap creepy fun!"
—Aaron Reynolds, author of *Creepy Carrots*

"Here's to hoping *Halloween Costume Caper* becomes a movie."
—*Reel Girl*

"I didn't want this Halloween adventure to end."
—*Fright Bites*

"Kat is a great character for young girls to look to; she faces problems like bullying and feeling insignificant, but she's strong, courageous, and a leader."
—*Sare-endipity*

Kat McGee and The School of Christmas Spirit

A Kat McGee Adventure

Book 1

Rebecca Munsterer

In This Together Media

New York, New York

For Ben Gentine, who dreams of Christmas morning

CHAPTER 1

Kat McPee. It didn't get much worse than that.

Katherine Elizabeth McGee was her full name. Kat always thought it sounded like the name of a princess. But nobody called her Katherine. They just called her Kat.

And the "McPee" nickname wasn't Kat's fault. After all, the accident happened four years ago, when she was only in the first grade. Everyone knows that first graders are *expected* to have accidents. But most first graders don't have to live with their mistakes for the rest of their lives.

It all started when Kat drank a super-sized, freshly-squeezed lemonade at the Town Carnival right before her oldest sister dared her to ride the Rocket Roller Coaster.

Kat's siblings knew that she was afraid of heights. The Rocket Roller Coaster towered over the carnival, calling itself the "tallest loop-the-loop" in the Northern Hemisphere. Kat would have laughed off the dare, but as her other siblings joined in the teasing, she knew she had something to prove. Even her little brother Gus, who stood on his tippy toes to pass the height requirement for the ride, was boarding. If Gus could do it, so could she.

Squaring her shoulders, Kat boarded the coaster with her six siblings. Many of her classmates were watching from the fairgrounds below. When the Rocket took off, Kat closed her eyes and tried to be brave.

But with all of that lemonade swishing around in her belly, she couldn't help herself.

Kat wet her pants.

Ever since that incident four years ago, everyone in Totsville, Maine called her "Kat McPee." It was bad enough to have an accident on a roller coaster, but it was even worse to have a nickname that stuck like glue.

None of Kat's other brothers and sisters ever had to live with a terrible nickname. In fact, they were perfect children; their awards, certificates, and trophies lined the wall of the McGee home. Hannah McGee, Kat's older sister, won the town spelling bee seven times in a row. Abe McGee, her youngest brother, was the best Little League baseball player in the state. Emily McGee was a prize-winning violinist; Polly McGee had her brown belt in karate. Ben McGee was the state mini-golf champion, and Gus McGee could say "thank you" in seven languages—eight, if you included English.

Kat had never received a special award. She was always in the audience, on the sidelines, or behind the scenes. And being the middle child made her feel even more totally, completely average. Her siblings made up a theme song about their sister:

"Her underpants are yellow.

She always gets B's.

Her stomach's like Jello.

Here comes Kat McPee!"

While the song hurt, it wasn't all wrong. Her white underpants somehow came out of the wash with a yellowish tint. Her stomach *was* a little wobbly. And as for the B's—they were being nice. She'd been known to bring home a C from time to time.

Kat even played the recorder "with average talent," according to her music teacher. While all of her classmates had moved on to "Up on the Housetop," Kat was still trying to master "Hot Cross Buns."

Being average took its toll on poor Kat. Her only friends were her two cats, Salt and Pepper, whom she counted on for companionship after school. Spending time with Salt and Pepper was Kat's favorite part of the day, yet she couldn't help but feel lonely every once in a while.

So, in fifth grade, Kat decided to reinvent herself. If she was going to drop the "Kat McPee" nickname before entering the new world of middle school, Kat knew that she had to be better than average at something.

So she set her sights on the Totsville Christmas Pageant.

The Totsville Christmas Pageant was famous. The largest holiday event of the year, it was bigger than the Totsville Fourth of July Parade. It was more spectacular than the Totsville Valentine's Day Formal Dance. It was even more special than the Totsville Father's Day Fishing Tournament. The Christmas Pageant was such a big deal that the Totsville Drugstore, which prided itself on being open 365 days a year, 24 hours a day, actually closed for ONE hour during the pageant so that the drugstore employees could attend.

Mary was the most coveted part in the pageant. Every November, Principal Pratt picked a fifth-grade girl to play the role, and this year, Kat was desperate to be chosen. The competition was tough, considering that there were exactly twenty-seven other girls in Kat's class, and everybody wanted the part. But Kat had a competitive advantage. All three of her older sisters had played Mary. Kat had studied their every move, from how to sit properly on the donkey to the right way to carry the baby Jesus.

Plus, she had spent all fall growing out her mousy brown hair, knowing that Principal Pratt typically chose long-haired girls to don Mary's veil. Kat's normally shoulder-length hair was now long enough to reach her belly button.

On the Friday before Thanksgiving week, the names of the pageant players were revealed at a Totsville Elementary School assembly. Kat wore her lucky purple shirt and sat in the front row so that Principal Pratt was sure to remember her.

The role of Joseph was announced first. Soccer star John Jennings was picked. The students clapped as John walked to the front of the auditorium to stand next to Principal Pratt.

"The next pageant player I will announce is the role of Mary," Principal Pratt said.

Kat took a deep breath and closed her eyes.

"It was a very difficult decision, but after much deliberation, I decided to go with the girl with the very long hair," Principal Pratt continued.

Kat opened her eyes and grinned widely. *So long, Kat McPee,* she thought.

"I'm proud to announce that the next Mary will be … Molly Mudge!" Principal Pratt said.

Kat slouched down in her seat. She couldn't believe her ears. Molly Mudge? Molly Mudge's hair was shorter than Kat's, and Molly didn't have any experience with the pageant. In fact, Molly Mudge didn't even attend last year's pageant, because she had the chicken pox.

The class clapped. Kat scowled.

As the assembly progressed, things actually got worse! Kat wasn't cast for *any* role in the pageant. Not an angel. Not a shepherd. Not even a lousy caroler.

She decided to approach the Principal directly, and went to her office later in the afternoon.

"Principal Pratt, I don't mean to complain, but I don't understand how I wasn't picked to be Mary," Kat said. "I have the longest hair in the entire fifth grade."

"Yes, dear," the Principal said, "but it's *curly*." Principal Pratt ran her finger through one of Kat's curls. "We all know that we *can't* have a curly-haired Mary. It wouldn't be right."

"Excuse me, Principal Pratt," the Principal's assistant interrupted, peering out from behind the office door. "Molly Mudge's father is here to see you."

"Send him in," Principal Pratt said. "Now, Kat, you need to go back to class."

Determined not to let Principal Pratt see her cry, Kat ran out of the office. As she turned the corner by the door, she slammed into Mr. Mudge and knocked his briefcase from his hand.

"Watch where you're going, young lady!" Mr. Mudge screamed.

Principal Pratt came out of her office, alarmed. "Kat McGee! You're always getting in the way!"

"I'm sorry," Kat apologized, tears streaming down her face.

Kat and Principal Pratt helped Mr. Mudge pick up the scattered papers from his briefcase. As Kat gathered a few papers, she picked up an unsealed white envelope. It was addressed to Principal Pratt, and it was filled with cash.

"Wow," Kat said aloud to Mr. Mudge. "Why are you giving Principal Pratt all of this money?"

"Shh!" Mr. Mudge swiped the envelope from Kat's hand.

"That's none of your business," Principal Pratt announced. "Now, go back to class immediately."

That afternoon on the school bus, Kat confided in her sisters about the money in the envelope.

"I think it was a bribe," she whispered. "I think Mr. Mudge paid Principal Pratt to pick his daughter for the pageant."

"Kat, don't be such a liar," Hannah replied.

"Yeah, Kat," Emily said. "It's bad enough that you weren't chosen for *any* part in the pageant. Now you're making up stories to make yourself feel better."

"But I'm telling you what I saw with my own eyes," Kat pleaded.

"Nobody will believe you, Kat. You're a nobody. And no one is going to listen to a nobody," Hannah said.

"Do yourself a favor, Kat," Polly proclaimed, "and don't embarrass yourself more. Just keep your mouth shut and *try* to be normal. You're always making the rest of us look bad."

A few weeks later, on December 17th, the townsfolk of Totsville gathered for the annual Christmas pageant. Principal Pratt arrived at the pageant wearing a brand new diamond necklace.

"See," Kat said to her sister, Hannah, pointing to the Principal. "Principal Pratt didn't have that fancy necklace before this pageant."

"Hush," Hannah ordered. "I told you that nobody believes you, Kat. If you say one more word, I'm going to tell Mom and Dad that you're making up stories because you're a loser."

Kat watched the rest of the pageant in silence. The audience cheered for Kat's classmates when they paraded out dressed as shepherds and carolers and angels. But nobody cheered for Kat, who stood alone in the audience.

That evening, when Kat arrived home after the pageant, she saw an unusual car parked in the driveway. Her heart leapt. The license plate read "BELIEVE"—an instant giveaway.

"Gram McGee!" Kat screamed as she ran into the house.

Gram McGee was the only person on Earth who believed Kat was special. Gram and Pops McGee lived across the country in Seattle, but every year they came to stay with the McGee family for the week before Christmas. In her devastation over the Christmas Pageant, Kat had completely forgotten about Gram's visit.

"Hello, my precious Kat!" Gram greeted her.

Kat gave Gram a hug, breathing in her signature smell: peppermint and evergreen trees. "Hi Gram!"

"You're right on time," Gram said. "I was about to start baking my smashed sweet potatoes, and I need a helper. Your grandfather is in the backyard playing flag football with your sisters and brothers. I was hoping I could count on you."

It was nice to be needed. Just seeing Gram made Kat forget about Principal Pratt and the rigged pageant. "Count me in!" Kat replied.

Kat and Gram spent the afternoon cooking. Gram even shared her secret ingredient (a sprinkle of cinnamon) for her famous smashed sweet potatoes, though she made Kat promise not to tell her siblings.

"Mrs. Claus taught me about the wonders of cinnamon," Gram said.

"Mrs. Claus?" Kat echoed. "*The* Mrs. Claus?"

"Of course," Gram laughed. "What other Mrs. Claus is there?"

"But how do you know her?" Kat asked as she peppered the sweet potatoes.

"Sadie and I went to high school together," Gram said. "We loved books, so we formed our own Varsity Book Team to get recognition for all of our speed reading."

Kat wondered if her grandmother had been drinking too much eggnog. "You went to high school with Mrs. Claus?"

"Sure," Gram said, "She's a great gal! We still keep in touch come holiday time." Gram laughed and added, "She certainly sends the best Christmas cards."

For the rest of the evening, as Kat and Gram cooked in the kitchen, Kat listened to Gram's stories about her beloved friend, Sadie Claus. Kat liked the stories, but couldn't help but wonder if Gram was pulling her leg.

"It sounds a little unbelievable, Gram," Kat said with a smile.

"People who believe in the unbelievable live unbelievably wonderful lives," Gram whispered. "By the way," she said, twirling one of Kat's curls in her fingers, "you look so pretty with long hair."

That night, Kat prepared for bed, her tummy full of Gram's famous smashed sweet potatoes. She brushed her teeth. She said goodnight to her grandparents. And she gave Salt and Pepper their nightly kisses.

As Kat made her way to her tiny bed in the corner of the fourth floor of the McGee household, she noticed something sparkly on her pillow. Picking up the object, she realized it was a snow globe with a small village scene inside. Kat smiled to herself, guessing that it was a present from Gram. She twirled the globe and gave it a good shake. Tiny flakes of snow fell over the miniature village.

As Kat marveled at the swirling snow, she started to feel a little off-balance. She shook her head, and concentrated on the globe. Strangely, she still felt drowsy. Blinking her eyes slowly, she reclined on the bed, snow globe in hand.

Her eyes closed while the snow in the globe still fell …

CHAPTER 2

"You look just like your Gram."

The voice swam into Kat's mind as she opened her eyes. A strange elderly woman with silver hair and pink lips smiled sweetly at Kat. She wore a red velvet coat with white trim and small black-rimmed glasses.

"You even have her dimples," the woman said.

Kat sat up sharply. She was in an unfamiliar chair in an equally unfamiliar room. As she looked around, she realized that she was no longer in the McGee house. What had happened? Kat blinked and refocused on the stranger, who sat at a nearby desk.

"I'm sorry," Kat said. "Do I know you?"

"We've never met formally but I'm a friend of your grandmother's," the woman said. "I'm Sadie. Sadie Claus."

I MUST still be sleeping, Kat thought. She took her left hand and pinched her right forearm, hoping to wake up.

"Oh dear little one, you're not dreaming," Mrs. Claus said. "But you sure are a lovely young lady, aren't you?"

Kat smiled at Mrs. Claus. She'd called her lovely. *Nobody* ever called Kat lovely, except her Gram. She must be far from Totsville, Kat thought, where everyone called her Kat McPee.

"You've been nominated for a very coveted position, and I'm happy to say that you're the final transport of the day," Mrs. Claus continued.

"Transport?" Kat asked.

"No time to explain," Mrs. Claus said, looking down at her watch. "We must hurry. Orientation starts in five minutes! Follow me."

Kat followed Mrs. Claus out of the office into a winter wonderland. The landscape was snow-covered and looked remarkably similar to the scene in her snow globe.

"The North Pole," Kat whispered to herself.

"Stay close," Mrs. Claus said, "Since the Elf condominium expansion, things have gotten quite confusing around here. It's easy to get lost if you don't pay attention."

Kat followed Mrs. Claus down a path. High snow walls loomed on either side. They passed a toyshop, a bakery and a post office. Everything in the North Pole was a bit twinkly, a bit sparkly, and a bit beautiful. Each evergreen tree glistened with multi-colored lights. Silver ivy decorated the side of each building like winding ribbons. And every snowman wore a smile.

As they walked, Kat noticed the reindeer stables. Being an animal lover, she couldn't help herself. "May I take a peek?" she asked as she and Mrs. Claus strolled past a stable marked, "Dasher."

"Oh, all right," Mrs. Claus agreed.

Kat snuck up to the stable and peeked inside. A beautiful reindeer with pointy antlers thrust his nose out toward her. Kat reached forward to rub his snout. "He's spectacular," she said, awed.

"He is wonderful," Mrs. Claus agreed as she lovingly scratched the reindeer's nose. "Now, we don't have another moment to waste. Let's get going."

Kat followed Mrs. Claus to the tallest building she'd seen yet, which sat right smack in the middle of the North Pole. A granite engraving that read "The School of Spirit, Est. 856," was carved on its main wall.

Mrs. Claus stopped by a massive oak door at the front of the building.

"Are you ready, Kat?" she asked.

Kat nodded. She didn't know what exactly she was ready for. But she knew that she was.

Slowly, Mrs. Claus pushed the door open, revealing a cathedral-sized room filled with fidgety children. The children, all about Kat's age, were dressed in pajamas and nightgowns. They perched on cherry wood benches, seemingly awaiting some sort of speaker. When Mrs. Claus entered, their mumbles and grumbles quickly quieted.

Mrs. Claus walked towards the podium in front of the students. Kat took the only empty seat in the hall. It was a front row seat next to a young boy with tousled hair and somewhat tattered pajamas.

"Good evening, children," Mrs. Claus said.

"Good evening, Mrs. Claus," the children answered.

"As we say in the North Pole, welcome to the tip-top place in the world … The School of Christmas Spirit!" Mrs. Claus smiled. "You children have been chosen by one of The Nominators to rehabilitate your spirit at our home. We know that you have potential, so we're here to let your spirit shine! Now, I'd like to introduce some of our special guests this evening …"

Ten Elves, all elderly in appearance but childlike in disposition, marched in single file down the middle aisle. The seated children gasped in amazement. Kat pinched her forearm again just to be sure she wasn't dreaming. The boy seated next to her whispered, "I thought Elves were only imaginary!"

Mrs. Claus continued her speech. "During your stay, our Elves will be your teachers, mentors, and chaperones. Little boys will room in the Puppy Dog Tails Dorm, and little girls will room in Sugar and Spice. The Elves will help take care of you during your time at the North Pole."

Kat smiled. The School of Christmas Spirit sounded like an interesting place. She'd never had an Elf friend before, and people here didn't know that her name back home was Kat *McPee.*

"And without further ado," Mrs. Claus continued, "I'd like to introduce our Assistant Headmaster and CEO, Chief Elf of Operations, Scoogie. Edward "Scoogie" Claus is a graduate of the Wintergreen Business Academy, and the two-time winner of the Golden Goose Award for excellence in management. He's also the cousin of my husband, which makes him not only a work colleague, but family as well. He will present the rules of the school."

The tallest of the tiny Elves stepped forward and took his place at the podium. His whitish hair peeked out from under a red cap. (All of the other elves wore green caps.) He had long, slender fingers, and a pointy triangular nose. He looked like he could afford to gain a few pounds, Kat thought. She could probably blow him over with a feather.

"Hello, class," Scoogie squeaked. "As the CEO of The School of Christmas Spirit, I welcome you on behalf of the Elfhood."

The Elves clapped enthusiastically.

Scoogie continued, "The School of Christmas Spirit is a distinguished institution, established in 856 AD by our beloved patron, Sadie Claus. We have educated some of the finest world leaders, such as the honorable Martin Luther King, Jr., the kind-hearted Mother Teresa, and the pop icon Barry Manilow. We take our spirit education seriously and tolerate no mischief from our students. Now, please reach under your seat and pick up The School of Christmas Spirit Contract."

Kat reached under the bench and found a contract taped to the wood. She tugged it free and started to read:

The School of Christmas Spirit Contract
1. *Pencils must always be No. 2 Pencils. (Santa is allergic to Number 1, and Numbers 3- 108).*
2. *Cookies MUST be dunked in milk before they are eaten.*

3. *No reindeer games ... ever.*
4. *Students must wear purple jumpsuits so that they are easily recognized as non-Elves.*
5. *Absolutely, positively, no saying the "S" word.*

"What's the S word?" Kat whispered to the boy next to her. He shrugged.

Scoogie overheard Kat's question and walked towards her. "For those of you who do not know the S word, it is the place which is the exact opposite of the North Pole."

"The Sou..." Kat started.

"Hush," Scoogie said with a forgiving smile. "My dear child, the S word is a horrible place. While the North Pole is filled with good will and wonder, the S word is filled with jealousy and greed. Growing up there, Santa was surrounded by people whose hearts were filled with anger. When my parents, his aunt and uncle, saved Santa from the S word and brought him to the North Pole, we all decided that we would never mention the S word again."

Kat nodded respectfully and continued to read:

6. *Lastly, each member of The School of Christmas Spirit must solemnly swear that he/she will never, ever, speak of his/her experience to ANYONE outside of the North Pole.*

Kat borrowed a Number 2 pencil from the girl on the bench behind her, and signed the contract. Scoogie collected the documents, nodding his head in satisfaction. Smiling, Mrs. Claus returned to the podium.

"To graduate, class, you must display an understanding of The Four Tenets of Spirit: worthiness, wonder, will, and whimsy. You will be pushed through intensive training on the Tenets, and then you will have to complete a final project."

Kat looked around as Mrs. Claus spoke. The audience was a mishmash of eccentric-looking kids. Kat counted the children. Twenty-four misfits—including Kat. One boy was picking his nose. Another girl wore a nightgown covered with pineapples. And one girl had five pigtails popping out of different spots on her head.

"We shall commence this evening and reconvene in the morning," Mrs. Claus concluded. "At promptly 9 AM, children, please report to Nicholas Library for your first lesson. Wear your purple jumpsuits and be sure to eat the morning breakfast, which will be delivered to your room. It promises to be a long day, and you'll need your vitamins."

Kat followed a line of girls to the Sugar and Spice Dorm. Her room was simple, with a small white bed and a closet full of purple jumpsuits.

As she crawled into bed, Kat pinched herself one last time. She hoped that she *wasn't* dreaming, but she wanted to make sure. She was excited to be far away from home, away from the place where people knew her, away from Kat McPee.

CHAPTER 3

Kat awoke to the sound of a knock.

"Breakfast, Miss McGee," a voice called.

Opening her eyes, Kat looked around warily. She was still in her dorm room at the North Pole. With a sigh of relief, she hopped out of bed and opened the door. An Elf holding a platter of goodies smiled at her.

"Hi, I'm Chip, your Elf Concierge! Today's breakfast is candyfruit," he said. "Go ahead. Pick one."

Kat inspected the square-shaped, rainbow-colored fruits. "Candyfruit?" she asked. She had never seen anything like it.

"A North Pole delicacy," Chip smiled. "Certified organically grown in Mrs. Claus' garden."

Kat picked up a candyfruit and sniffed. It smelled like oranges and chocolate.

"Are you sure this is a fruit?"

"Absolutely," Chip responded. "It has a hundred percent of your daily Vitamin C. Plus Vitamin V for self-confidence, Vitamin X for willpower, Vitamin Y for your creativity … and Vitamin Z for a little luck."

18

Kat took a bite of the candyfruit and let her taste buds delight in the sweetness. "De-licious!" she exclaimed. Chip smiled and walked to the next room.

Minutes later, Kat joined a swarm of children on their way across campus to Nicholas Hall. She chatted with a few of the students in the back of the pack. Jackson from Texarkana, Texas, was the boy who'd sat next to Kat the previous day. He still looked like he hadn't brushed his hair.

"Where did you get those fancy pajamas yesterday?" he asked Kat.

"Fancy?" she asked.

"Yeah, fancy," he said. "All shiny and clean-looking."

"They were silk," Kat said. "My Gram gave them to me."

"Oh," Jackson said. "I've never seen silk pajamas. In fact, my pajamas have a lot of holes."

"At least you're cool at night," Kat said, and she and Jackson giggled.

Then, Kat chatted with Jillian, a girl from Detroit, who was the stepchild of the super famous rock musician Bruce Doogood. Jillian told Kat that she hadn't seen her father in five years because of his tour schedule.

"I'm an only child, so it gets pretty lonely around the house," Jillian confided to Kat.

"You're lucky," Kat said. "I have six brothers and sisters. I'm stuck in the middle."

"Six!" Jillian exclaimed. "My entire life, I've wanted even *one* sibling. I would give anything to have six! You could have your own family basketball team … with an extra player."

"If we did, I'd be the one on the bench," Kat frowned.

"It's better to be on the bench than to be all alone," Jillian said. "I'm happy just to be at this school … at least I have interesting people like you to talk to."

"Like me?" Kat asked. Her brothers and sisters had never considered Kat to be *interesting*.

"Sure," Jillian said. "You seem pretty cool."

Kat and her two new friends arrived at Nicholas Library only moments before the clock tower struck 9 AM. Mrs. Claus and Scoogie stood inside the doorway, waiting for the students.

"Come in, come in," Mrs. Claus said. "We'll be starting momentarily, so please make your way to the carpet."

Nicholas Library was an octagon-shaped building, and all eight sides were covered in books. The books were arranged by color: Red, Orange, Yellow, Green, Blue, Purple, Brown, and Black. All of the red books were on the north wall. All of the blue books were on the south wall. All of the yellow books were on the northeast wall of the building, while all of the green books were on the southwest wall. The building looked like a rainbow of knowledge.

A large white carpet lay in the middle of the floor. The boys and girls filed in and sat down on it in a semi-circle. The Totsville Library back home had only one shelf of children's books, Kat thought. Here, however, the entire orange wall was labeled, "For Fifth Graders Only." There must have been a thousand orange books, solely for readers her age. Kat marveled at the thought.

Mrs. Claus took to the center of the floor. Kat really admired Mrs. Claus, partly because she reminded Kat of her Gram, and partly because she displayed such self-confidence. Kat enjoyed watching her command the attention of the students, while also communicating deep and honest affection.

Mrs. Claus cleared her throat. "Boys and girls, today we will study the Tenet of Worthiness. Worthiness, or self-worth, is one of the most critical features of spirit. We must value ourselves before we can value anything else. And so, to kick-off your Christmas Spirit education, we've invited a celebrated guest speaker to discuss the importance of worthiness."

The door to the library opened, and a familiar face entered the room. It was Santa Claus himself. The children buzzed with excitement.

"Ho-Ho-Hello, boys and girls," Santa chortled.

"He looks even bigger in person," Kat whispered to Jillian.

Santa walked to the front of the semi-circle and pulled up a chair. He rubbed his white whiskers and squinted his eyes before pulling out a pair of tiny glasses. After putting the glasses on the end of his nose, he looked directly at the children.

"How many of you have ever felt unimportant?" he asked.

Kat slowly raised her hand. To her surprise, every other child raised his or her hand as well.

"Let me tell you a story about a young boy who also felt unimportant. This little boy grew up on the South Side of *the S word*. His parents neglected him. His friends teased him relentlessly for having white hair at the age of six. People told him that he was different. But in his heart, he felt like he was different *in a good way.*"

The children leaned in, fascinated by Santa's story.

"One day, that little boy went to a local carnival. The other kids continued to tease him relentlessly for his white hair and tattered clothing. After they refused to let him ride the tilt-a-whirl with them, the little boy ran away, crying. He reached the corner of the carnival and hid in an antique photo booth.

"As he cowered down in the booth, the camera flashed, taking the little boy by surprise. After a minute, a black-and white picture emerged from the camera. The little boy grabbed it. It was a picture of an older gentleman, wearing a red hat. He had the same white hair as the little boy. The man looked happy, and he was surrounded by smiling children. The little boy marveled at this vision of the future, and realized that he had worth in the world.

"He decided to live up to the potential of that image."

Santa stood up from his chair as Scoogie wheeled in an unknown object draped with a red velvet cover. Scoogie dramatically pulled the cover away, revealing an ornate gold-trimmed antique photo booth.

"The Photo Booth of Potential remains one of my most valuable possessions," Santa said. "I brought it here because I want to share it with you, boys and girls. Come, step in, and see the potential in yourselves."

The children assembled into a single-file line. Jackson was first. He took a deep breath and stepped into the booth. The students outside the photo booth saw a flash and heard him scream. After a moment of silence, Jackson exited the booth holding a black-and-white picture in his hand. It was a picture of a doctor.

"I've always liked pulling off bandages," Jackson said, and smiled.

Jillian was next. She walked up slowly, as if she wanted to inspect the actual photo booth before stepping inside. There was another flash, and Jillian exited the booth, grinning from ear to ear. She held up a picture of the Oval Office, complete with Jillian signing documents at the desk.

"The President?" she said in disbelief.

"That's the way it looks," Santa exclaimed. "Ladies and gentleman, please give a warm round of applause for our first female president, Jillian!"

The students clapped enthusiastically. They continued taking turns in the photo booth and exiting one by one, carrying photos. The pictured futures showed everything from dolphin trainers to firefighters, Olympic athletes to literary scholars. Each child marveled at his or her potential. Santa, Scoogie, and Mrs. Claus watched with delight.

Having hung back, Kat was the very last in line. She stepped into the photo booth slowly, nervous about her fate.

Inside the booth, a large sign read, "Smile … It's Your Future." Kat smiled, and was blinded by a flash. After a few seconds, a photograph popped out of the vending tray.

Kat picked up the photo—and screamed, almost dropping it. She was horrified. Slowly, she stepped out of the booth, knees shaking.

"Well?" Santa asked. Kat hid the photo behind her back.

"I'd rather not share," she said, looking down at the ground.

Mrs. Claus came to her side. "Oh, dear Kat, it can't be that bad."

Kat took a deep breath and slowly held up her photo. It was an image of Kat, riding on a sleigh, cheering on the reindeer. Mrs. Claus was at Kat's side in the picture, but Santa was nowhere to be seen.

"Well, that's strange," Santa said. "It looks like someone might take my place!"

Was she fated to become the next Santa Claus? Kat wondered. That was crazy!

Scoogie laughed out loud at Kat's picture. "I think there's been a malfunction," he said. "Here, let me give it a try."

Scoogie walked into the booth. A long moment passed. No flash.

"It's not doing anything," Kat said.

"Patience, please," Scoogie said, sticking his head out of the hole in the curtain. Turning, he slipped back inside. An instant later, there was a horrible crackling noise. The photo booth started to shake. Smoke puffed from the back of the booth as it rumbled and rocked. Finally, it stopped with a loud BOOM.

Mrs. Claus let out a gasp. "Scoogie, are you okay?"

Scoogie stepped out of the photo booth, embarrassed. "I'm fine," he said. "Clearly, this photo booth is defective."

Santa, though clearly disappointed about the broken booth, still came to Scoogie's side and patted Scoogie on the back.

"I'm just glad you're okay," he said.

The children spent the remainder of the afternoon listening to Santa's stories about building up his empire in the North Pole. Santa spoke for over six hours, although time passed so quickly that Kat felt like she had only been with Santa for minutes.

Santa peppered his lesson with personal anecdotes:

> *How he built his first toy with only a lump of clay … and a vision.*
>
> *How he adopted reindeer from a rescue shelter in the Subarctic.*
>
> *How he taught himself the physics behind building a flying sleigh.*
>
> *How he coined his trademark "Ho Ho Ho" after shortening his personal mantra: "Home with my Honey for the Holiday."*

At the end of the day, Mrs. Claus dismissed the children from the carpet, and encouraged them to spend the rest of the day reading books in the library.

As he left, Santa made one last stop. He walked over to Kat, who was perusing the myriad children's books on the orange shelf.

"Just so you know, Miss McGee," Santa said in his deep voice, "I couldn't think of a better replacement for me than you."

"Replacement?" Kat asked nervously. "Why do you need a replacement?"

Santa chuckled. "Well, I *am* getting older, and Mrs. Claus and I can't do this forever. Scoogie says there are great retirement communities in Fort Lauderdale … Mini-golf courses on every block! Can you imagine?"

"I don't even want to think about you retiring," Kat said. "What will the world do without Santa?"

"Well, young one," Santa put his hand on Kat's shoulder. "I appreciate the support. But if I do retire, I think you would do a swell job taking over."

With a wink to Kat and a wave to the other schoolchildren, Santa left the library.

Kat stood very still, perplexed. She couldn't imagine the North Pole without Santa and Mrs. Claus. Was she really the person fated to take over their empire?

CHAPTER 4

On her second day at The School of Christmas Spirit, Kat awoke to another knock on her door. She hopped from her bed, still in her pajamas, expecting another room service delivery of delicious candyfruit.

But when she opened the door, she was greeted by Chip, the concierge Elf – and no candyfruit platter.

"Morning, Miss McGee," Chip smiled.

"Good morning," Kat responded.

"I need your thumbs," Chip said.

"My thumbs?" Kat asked, looking down at her hands.

"Yep," Chip said. "Protocol for today's Tenet."

He presented a blue ink pad and a piece of paper. Kat took her thumbs, dipped them in the ink, and pressed them firmly onto the paper, leaving a print. As she rolled her fingers away, the blue ink magically turned red.

"Very good," Chip said. "You've passed the quality test." He carefully folded the paper and placed it in a folder. "Now, get dressed in your jumpsuit and meet the other students at building 123ABC. It's past the reindeer stables, but before the golf course."

A few minutes later, Kat walked across the North Pole campus, arriving at a triangular building marked 123ABC. A "DO NOT ENTER" sign was pasted to the front door.

One by one, the other kids arrived. Rumors that one of the students had failed the "quality test" were abuzz. Lucy Caruthers, who had been fighting the flu, had apparently given a thumbprint that never turned red. She'd been sent to the infirmary, while the rest of the students were cleared to proceed.

After the last student arrived, Mrs. Claus and Scoogie joined the group.

"Children," Mrs. Claus began. "Welcome to Building 123ABC, otherwise known as …" she put a finger to her lips and whispered, "Command Central."

The children sighed a collective *ooohhh*.

"Today," Mrs. Claus said, "we'll be learning about The Tenet of *Wisdom*. As we enter the building, please be sure to keep your germs to yourself. We cannot let any of the technology inside be infected with viruses. No sneezing. No coughing. No hiccupping. And absolutely, positively *no* nose picking."

Kat and the other students formed a line behind Mrs. Claus; Kat saw Jillian and Jackson behind her, and waved. Jackson gave her a blue thumbs-up.

Mrs. Claus pressed her thumb against a square pad near the revolving door, which started spinning. The thumbprint allowed access to the mysterious building, Kat realized. One by one, the students entered behind Mrs. Claus.

Command Central was triangular-shaped, and filled with steel cubicles. At each cubicle, an Elf in a business suit typed furiously at a computer. Scoogie and Mrs. Claus led the students to an area on the perimeter of the building marked "Viewing Room".

Inside, Scoogie stepped forward. "Welcome, children, to Command Central, the heart of operations here at the North Pole. From this room, our Corporate Elves monitor the business of all of the children in the world. They are distinguishing naughty from nice children, and estimating the cost of this year's Christmas based on the behavior of all the kids in the world."

Kat's eyes traveled to what seemed to be a giant scoreboard of "Naughty" and "Nice" children. The scoreboard hung over the cubicles, displaying large green numbers. The numbers changed every millisecond, constantly showing new data. After a minute of watching the scoreboard, Kat's eyes began to hurt.

"Our Corporate Elves have endured years of professional training,"Scoogie continued."All of them have MBAs—Masters of Behavior Analysis—and most have interned with Santa himself. We brought you here today to be paired up with a Corporate Elf. Your job will be to judge students and create your own Naughty and Nice portfolio."

Mrs. Claus and Scoogie assigned each student to a cubicle. Kat was assigned to 13, in the very corner of the room. She and the other students walked gingerly to their respective cubicles, careful not to disturb the working Elves or cough on any of the expensive-looking technology.

Cubicle 13 was decorated with a series of diplomas from Mistletoe University, all in ostentatiously large frames. Inside,

Kat was greeted by an Elf who wore a monocle over one eye and spoke with a British accent.

"You must be the intern," he said in an unfriendly manner.

"Yes, hello," Kat said, taking a seat next to the Elf. "I'm Kat."

"That's an animal name," he said, unimpressed. "My name is George, but you can call me Mr. Nickel." Mr. Nickel was not interested in pleasantries, Kat thought, shifting uncomfortably in her chair. "Let's get to work, shall we?"

"Yes, George," Kat said. "I mean, um, Mr. Nickel!"

On Mr. Nickel's desk, a larger than life computer screen flickered to life at the touch of a button. "This is my PXMAS1225 computer," the Elf said. "It will display pictures of children from around the world. When you see someone who you feel should be placed on the NICE list, simply press the 'Enter' button, and the computer will calculate the investment. When you see someone who should be classified as NAUGHTY, press the 'X'."

"Sounds easy enough," Kat said, concentrating on the screen. Mr. Nickel snickered; Kat ignored him.

The first image appeared. It was a picture of a young boy playing fetch with his father in a baseball field. Kat pressed ENTER.

"Very good," Mr. Nickel said.

The next image was a picture of a girl eating rice at a kitchen table. The girl offered some rice to her younger sister, and they took turns tasting the meal.

Kat pressed ENTER again.

"Nicely done," Mr. Nickel said.

Twenty images flashed across the screen in rapid succession. Children, helping their parents after school. Students doing the dishes or playing sports with their siblings. Kat pressed ENTER for all of them.

"This is easy," she said.

And then a new image appeared. It was Kat's younger brother, Abe.

Abe had teased Kat for her entire life. He was by far the brattiest of her siblings.

Mr. Nickel saw Kat hesitate. "Well?" he asked. "Don't pause for too long. The computer freezes after ten seconds."

On the screen, Kat watched her brother's movements. Abe was sneaking around Kat's room, fishing for something in her closet. He pulled out Kat's hidden piggy bank and shook it upside down until some quarters and wadded-up dollar bills fell to the ground.

"My allowance!" Kat gasped.

Abe slipped the money into his pocket, a sneaky smile on his face. He carefully put the piggy bank back in the closet.

"You'd better hurry and make a decision," Mr. Nickel said. "Five seconds. Four – three – two…"

Kat pressed the "X' button. She leaned back, upset with herself for placing her own brother on the Naughty list. But Mr. Nickel looked pleased with her selection.

"That was a wise decision. That boy looked like trouble."

"But he's not trouble," Kat blurted out. "He's my brother."

Mr. Nickel raised an eyebrow. "Interesting," he said. "Well, it looks like your brother will be quite disappointed come Christmas morning."

Kat didn't want her brother to be labeled as Naughty. Abe was a relentless teaser, but Kat knew that, deep down, he had a good heart. Rising slowly to her feet, Kat found the strength inside herself to speak up.

"Mr. Nickel, I don't want to do this anymore," she said.

"Excuse me, young lady?" Mr. Nickel asked.

Kat furrowed her brow. "It doesn't feel right to label people based on a ten-second video. There's so much more to a person than that. I'm sorry, but I can't continue."

Mr. Nickel smiled. "Congratulations, Kat," he said. "You just passed the Tenet of Wisdom."

Kat was confused. "I did?"

Mr. Nickel reached over and pinned a gold star to the collar of her purple jumpsuit.

"The Command Central exercise is a test of inner wisdom," he said. "And you recognized the truth. You *can't* label people based on a few seconds of their life. You need to get to know someone's inner self over time."

Kat smiled, proud of herself for speaking up. Surely that was above average.

"The Naughty and Nice list is actually determined by a full year's observation of every child on Earth," Mr. Nickel continued. He pressed a button on his computer keyboard, and the screen image changed. Four different squares, featuring four different children, appeared on his monitor. Kat recognized one of the children as Abe.

"See," Mr. Nickel said, pointing to the screen. "These are my four case studies for the year: Beth, Carey, Daniel, and your brother, Abe. I've been keeping an eye on all four of them. On Christmas Eve, I'll report their overall behavior to Santa, and they will be placed on either the Naughty or Nice list based on the entire YEAR."

"You watch them for three hundred and sixty-five days?" Kat asked.

Mr. Nickel nodded. "And there's hope for Abe yet. Last week, he actually PUT quarters in your piggy bank for hiding purposes. Today, he was taking them back so he could buy your mother a Christmas present."

Kat breathed a sigh of relief and looked at her gold star pin. "I feel much better."

Mr. Nickel smiled at Kat. "You used your intuition to make a statement about something important. That's wisdom!" He motioned toward the viewing room. "Now, go back to Mrs. Claus. Your lesson is over for the day."

Kat gave Mr. Nickel a hug and made her way back to the viewing room. To Kat's delight, every one of her classmates was already there, each proudly displaying a gold star. They too possessed wisdom far greater than they'd originally known.

That evening, after a dinner of peppermint-crusted chicken and sweet green beans, the students returned to their dorms for bedtime. As Kat started to change into her pajamas, she realized that her gold star pin was gone, and decided to retrace her steps in an effort to find it.

Sneaking out of her doom room, Kat made her way back to the dining hall. Her gold star pin lay on the floor underneath the table. Picking it up, Kat quickly exited —and saw Mrs. Claus and Scoogie walking down the hall. She hid behind a curtain, not wanting to be caught out of her room after curfew.

Mrs. Claus and Scoogie were speaking intensely as they walked by Kat. She couldn't help but overhear.

"Sadie, I'm concerned about him," Scoogie said. "Did you watch him this morning at breakfast? He put salt in his coffee instead of sugar! I know it's only a little mistake, but there have been lots of little mistakes lately. Taking the wrong vitamins. Calling the reindeer by the wrong names. Losing his reindeer reins. He seems more and more forgetful."

"Oh, Scoogie, my husband just has a lot on his mind. He always gets a bit forgetful around Christmas. He has so much on his plate."

Scoogie put his hand on Mrs. Claus' shoulder. "I know it's hard for you to admit, but you can talk to me. I'm family. Santa's not a spring chicken anymore, and I'm worried that as he gets older, he'll begin to be a liability around here. Retirement is a wonderful option."

Scoogie and Mrs. Claus walked on, their voices fading as they moved down the hallway. When the coast was clear, Kat ran back to her dorm room and locked the door.

She fell asleep, hoping that Scoogie was wrong about Santa's forgetfulness.

CHAPTER 5

The next morning, Kat awoke to a tap on her door. The clock on the wall read 5 AM. Kat rolled over on her pillow, sure that she had just *imagined* the door tap at this early hour.

The knock was louder the second time.

"Who is it?" Kat yelled, slightly frightened. Her window was dark, and she knew that it couldn't possibly be time for breakfast.

"It's me, Chip!" The Concierge Elf shouted. "Get up, get dressed, and get to the bakery. Bring the flashlight in your nightstand! You'll need it to make your way across campus."

Minutes later, Kat was stumbling across the dark, cold North Pole. All of the buildings around her were dark, with the exception of the bakery. A beacon of light, the bakery emitted a soft glow through its windows, calling Kat to its doors.

When she entered, Kat was surprised to find a lively scene at a very early hour. The bakery was buzzing! Elves in aprons scurried across the floor, carrying muffin tins, rolling pins, and bags of flour. On the first floor, huge metal mixers swirled ingredients in giant silver bowls; on the second floor, red pipes zigzagged around the walls, dumping ingredients and occasionally whistling with a burst of hot steam.

Mrs. Claus, Scoogie, and the other students stood near the front of the bakery, marveling at the scene. Pastries, strudels and cakes whirled by on a conveyor belt. There were donuts drizzled with pink frosting and danishes covered in blue sprinkles. The smell of baked goods permeated the air with essence of vanilla, cinnamon and sugar.

Kat had always loved baking with her grandmother, but she had never experienced a bakery like this. She marveled at all of the utensils, ovens, and tubes of frosting. For a second, she really missed her grandmother; Gram would love this place. Imagine the recipes she could learn!

Jillian and Jackson stepped closer to Kat. All three students gazed at a homemade apple pie with peppermint crust.

"This is NOTHING like the Dipping Donuts in my town," Jackson whispered.

Mrs. Claus clapped her hands, calling for attention. "Good morning, class. I hope you're all feeling awake and energized at 5 AM. Today promises to be a busy day."

Kat tried to stifle a yawn. As much as she loved baking, she sure didn't love being awake at this hour.

"A good baker adds the proper amount of sugar," Mrs. Claus continued, smiling at the children. "A great baker adds the proper amount of early morning sunlight. Our Baking

Elves rise at five each day to prepare scrumptious baked goods for the North Pole. The candyfruit muffins must be baked by 6 AM for Santa. Carrot cake is delivered to the reindeer by 6:30 AM, and gingerbread bagels are served in the dining hall to the rest of the Elves at 7 AM sharp."

"Gingerbread bagels?" Jillian whispered to Kat. "I've never heard of such a thing!"

"I think they sound delicious," Kat replied, licking her lips.

"Today's Tenet," Mrs. Claus said, "is about wonder. Wonder is curiosity in its purest form. It's what you feel when you look up at the night stars. It's what you think of when you watch a caterpillar turn into a butterfly. It is the essence of spirit that makes us try new things and take chances."

Scoogie stepped to the front of the group. "Your challenge today is to use your creativity, invention, and imagination to make something spectacular."

He clapped his hands loudly and nodded at the Head Baking Elf. Twelve Baking Elves carefully wheeled an incredibly large, peculiarly- shaped table to the middle of the bakery. The table held a series of lumpy objects, all hidden by a red and white striped blanket.

Scoogie dramatically pulled the blanket aside, exposing hundreds of bottles, pans, and cups of differently-labeled ingredients. Kat read a few of the labels: gummy worms, mincemeat, pineapple, rigatoni, and Greek yogurt.

"Children, here are 'the Ingredients of the World.' On this table is a sampling of every taste on the planet." Scoogie lifted one of the spoons and tasted it. "Chocolate milk," he said.

He lifted another and took a lick. "Miso soup." Yet another. "Peanut butter. They are all here, and they are all yours for the taking and … the baking."

"Your task today, boys and girls, will be to design your own signature Christmas cookie," Mrs. Claus said. "We don't want you to plan, nor do we want you to follow a recipe. We want you to explore your own interests … and find your own path to the most delicious creation. The possibilities are endless! The chocolate chip cookie, the brownie, and the peach pie were all invented in this bakery many years ago by students who rediscovered their own magic in The School of Christmas Spirit."

Responding to her words, the students quickly gathered around the table, carefully filling their arms with cups and spoons of ingredients. Jillian stuck with fruit flavors. Jackson loaded up on different types of sugary cereal. Other students grabbed everything from broccoli to cheddar cheese.

Kat stood, helpless before the overwhelming pile of flavors. After a while, Mrs. Claus approached her.

"Not sure where to start?"

Kat shook her head. "I bake a lot with Gram when she visits, but it's a little intimidating when I'm not even sure what I'm making."

"But that's the wonder of it, sweetheart!" Mrs. Claus said. "Do you know that your grandmother's biggest mistake in the kitchen accidentally created her most delicious meal? She spilled brown sugar in some ketchup years ago, and developed a recipe for barbecue sauce."

Kat loved Gram's barbecue sauce. Squaring her shoulders, she decided that if her grandmother could make the most out of a curious kitchen situation, so could she. Closing her eyes, Kat randomly chose four cups from the pile of ingredients. Looking down, she saw four distinctly different items:

Cinnamon.
Seedless watermelon chunks.
Crumbled banana bread.
Sea Salt.

Kat carried her ingredients to a nearby baking station. Mrs. Claus watched as she mixed them in a bowl with some flour and butter. The mixture turned many colors, from purple to red to yellow. Kat had never seen such colorful dough in her life.

"Well," Mrs. Claus said. "Aren't you going to taste it?"

Kat picked up a tiny piece of dough and put it in her mouth. "It needs a little something," she said. "Something … sweet. But also something savory."

"Perhaps some chopped candyfruit?" Mrs. Claus suggested.

Kat nodded. Grabbing a mug full of candyfruit, she added it to her mixture and dipped her finger in the dough again. It tasted like sunshine on a warm beach day. Kat was shocked. "It's delicious," she exclaimed.

"Of course it is, dear," Mrs. Claus announced. "It was baked by a McGee. The McGees are famous for their creativity—and the wonder of their spirit."

Mrs. Claus winked as she walked away from the table. Kat continued to stir her "Salted Cinna-Water-Nana Cookie" batter; after rolling the dough into small balls, she popped them in the oven and smiled to herself. Gram would be proud.

At that moment, one of the Baking Elves screamed across the bakery.

"Mrs. Claus, Mrs. Claus, come quick! It's the candy canes! The Christmas candy canes!"

Mrs. Claus and Scoogie ran over to the Baking Elf, who lifted a handful of candy canes in one shaking hand.

"Go ahead," the Baking Elf said, "taste them."

Mrs. Claus picked up a cane and stuck it in her mouth. She gagged. "That tastes horrible. Like mosquito wings. Like window cleaner. Like dirty laundry."

The Baking Elf nodded in agreement. "They ALL taste like this. All seventy-seven thousand candy canes! Ruined."

The bakery door swung open. Santa came running in.

"What happened?" He asked. "I heard yelling. Is everything okay?"

The Baking Elves quieted. One of the Elves whispered in Scoogie's ear; Scoogie nodded his head, looked down at his feet and then spoke on behalf of the group.

"Well, sir," Scoogie said. "Apparently, you didn't pay the sugar company bill last year, so this year they sent us cheap sugar, which couldn't hold up in our ovens. Our entire supply of this year's candy canes is spoiled."

"Of course I paid the sugar bill last year," Santa said. He reached into his pocket. "Why, I have the carbon copy of the check right here in my checkbook."

Scoogie scoffed for a second. "No offense, sir," he said. "But a carbon copy of the check? Most people pay online with credit cards these days."

"Call me old-fashioned," Santa said, "but this is how I do things."

"Fine, fine," Scoogie said. "Just show us the confirmation you received for the check. The proof of payment?"

"Confirmation?" Santa asked. "Proof? I never get anything like that. I just mailed out the check and figured Booger's Sugar Company received it."

"With all due respect, sir," Scoogie said, walking over to Santa, "we really need to upgrade to a more technological system in the North Pole. As I've been telling you, online accounting will prevent these mistakes."

Mrs. Claus looked down at her feet sheepishly. "Honey, I'm sure that you sent the check. It probably got lost in the mail. I think this is all just a misunderstanding." She laughed nervously. "It's not like we have to cancel Christmas because of a few sour candy canes. Now, let's get back to our baking, shall we?"

The Baking Elves continued their morning duties while the students finished their Christmas cookie preparation. As Kat pulled her cookies out of the oven, she glanced over at Santa. He was flipping through his checkbook, and he looked sad and disheartened. Kat decided to share one of her golden-brown cookies with him. Picking up the treat, Kat walked to the corner of the bakery.

"I brought you something, Santa," Kat said. "It's a Salted Cinna-Water-Nana cookie."

"Cookies always do cheer me up," Santa admitted. He took the cookie from Kat's outstretched hand and took a bite. "Delicious," he smiled. "I might be an old man, but I know a scrumptious Christmas cookie when I taste one!"

"I don't think you're an old man," Kat said. "In fact, I think you're still a kid at heart."

"I'm glad somebody does," Santa grinned. "Now go back to your cookies before the Elves gobble them up."

CHAPTER 6

After their early rising and long morning in the bakery, the students were exhausted. They'd created Christmas cookies, cleaned the entire kitchen, and helped Mrs. Claus reorganize the pile of "Ingredients of the World."

For once in her life, Kat was too tired and too full to enjoy lunch in the dining hall. Her Salted Cinna-Water-Nana cookies were so delicious that she'd eaten most of the batch at the bakery. The others she donated to the "Save the North Pole Penguin" food bank, receiving a hug from the attending Elf.

By 1 PM, Kat was ready for a nap. But there was no time for snoozing at The School of Christmas Spirit. Scoogie announced to the students that they all needed to report to building ABCD by 1:15 PM.

The good news for Kat was that building ABCD was the most celebrated location in the North Pole: the Toy Warehouse.

The Toy Warehouse was the grandest and most colorful building Kat had ever seen. It was ten stories high and organized into a cube. In the middle was a large lobby with views of the floors above. Each floor was organized by a "type" of toy.

Wooden toys on Floor Two. Dolls and dollhouses on Floor Three. Bicycles, skateboards, and pogo sticks on Floor Nine.

Mrs. Claus, Scoogie and the students stood in the lobby, heads lifted to the sky. They wondered at the diverse toy selection and the magnitude of all the gizmos and gadgets. There were remote-controlled cars, building blocks, and princess wands, train sets, dartboards, and xylophones. Kat was especially impressed by Floor Seven, which was filled with stuffed animals of every type, from teddy bears to tree frogs.

"Welcome to Santa's Toy Warehouse," Mrs. Claus began. "Here, we store the toys which are made all year in our workshops. The rocking horses are made in the woodshop; the pirate eye patches are made in the sewing shop. The puzzles are made in the jigsaw shop; the bubbles are made in our chemistry lab. There is something for everyone and everything for someone. And this is exactly the place to teach you about the last Tenet of spirit. The Tenet of Whimsy."

Mrs. Claus walked over to a nearby yo-yo, picked it up and began playing with it as she spoke.

"Whimsy is what happens when you allow yourself to be the person you are naturally. Whimsy is as silly as a grown-up who still loves playing with a yo-yo." To the surprise of the children, she cradled the yo-yo–then flipped it around and caught it back up in her hands. "I've spent at least one minute of every day of my life playing with a yo-yo. It reminds me of being a child. It reminds me of having balance in my life. It reminds me of good ol' fashioned fun."

Kat smiled fondly at Mrs. Claus. Although Mrs. Claus was an elderly woman, she had the spirit of a young girl like Kat.

"You, my dears, have worked incredibly hard in the past two days," Mrs. Claus said. "You have baked, you have studied, you have read, and you have listened. And now it's your time to play."

"Wheeeeee!" screamed all of the children.

"But before you get ahead of yourselves," Mrs. Claus said, continuing to yo-yo, "I have another announcement. I would like to introduce you to the Whimsy Elves."

Ten elves marched out to the center of the circle of students. Five wore light blue overalls. The other five wore dark blue overalls.

"Every year, the Whimsy Elves have an annual toy-building tournament, in which they stretch their imaginations to develop creative new toys for our workshop. They are engineers, artists, and dreamers by trade, and they are here today to give you personalized toy gifts to match your spirit."

"Toy gifts!" Jackson cheered. "Oh boy!"

One of the Whimsy Elves stepped forward and pulled a list from the pocket of his overalls. "Boys and girls, we believe that a toy is only as good as the child who plays with it. So, as the creators of these toys, we are honored to present specially chosen toys for each of your unique personalities."

Kat's eyes opened wide as she smiled at the mysterious Elves.

The Whimsy Elf cleared his throat and read from his list. "For Jillian, a paint set, to celebrate her creativity and inspired vision."

Jillian accepted her paint set with a smile.

"For Jackson, a boomerang, for his energy and his ability to bounce back from any situation."

Jackson ran to the Whimsy Elf and thanked him for his gift.

The Whimsy Elf continued gifting toys to all of the students. "And last, we have Kat McGee. For her love of the animal kingdom, we have a very special present … her own toy reindeer."

Kat accepted the stuffed animal. It looked exactly like one of Santa's pets. Picking it up, she said out loud, "I think I'll call you *Antlers*."

The Whimsy Elf concluded his presentation with a special message to the students. "Now, boys and girls, always continue dreaming and exploring, creating and innovating. For the magic of toys is the magic of imagination."

Scoogie nodded in approval at the Whimsy Elf 's words, cleared his throat, and stepped in front of the group. "Thank you for that heartwarming display. But before we leave the Toy Workshop, I too have a presentation."

Mrs. Claus looked surprised. "You do?"

Scoogie nodded and pulled a whistle-flute out of his pocket. He walked to the front of the Toy Workshop, opened the door, and played a ten-note tune to the air outside.

It took only seconds for Santa to appear.

"What's this all about?" Santa asked Scoogie. "I heard the emergency whistle."

"Sir," Scoogie said, trembling with excitement. "I am proud to announce that today we received a very important delivery."

Scoogie reached into his pocket and pulled out a small brown package. He gave it to Santa. "I've been waiting all day to give it to you. Go ahead. Open it."

The Whimsy Elves, the children, and Mrs. Claus all leaned in as Santa peeled away the brown packaging. A small, green glob of slime lay in his hand.

"I don't understand," Santa said. "What exactly IS it?"

Jackson, still clutching his boomerang, ran over to Santa. His eyes widened as he leaned in to inspect the slime. "It's a Blob!"

"A what?" the lead Whimsy Elf asked.

Jackson snatched the Blob from Santa's hand. "It's the newest, truest toy on the market! It hasn't even been released yet. You can use it to gross out your teachers and friends." Jackson turned to Scoogie. "How did you get one?"

"Well, I called my friend who works at the Slime Factory. He gave me one." Scoogie rolled out a long beige colored scroll. "I was curious to see it, since the Blob *is* the number one most requested Christmas toy this year."

Santa took the Blob back from Jackson and held it up, frowning. "This piece of gloop is the number one most requested toy? What happened to matchbox cars and jump ropes and rubber ducks?"

Scoogie shook his head. "Rubber Ducks were number 98,546 on the Most Wanted list. The Blob is first."

"But Scoogie," Mrs. Claus said sweetly, "we don't make Blobs here. And I'm sure that parents don't want their kids playing with such … such…"

"Mindless goop!" Santa interjected.

"Actually, Mrs. Claus," Scoogie continued, "The Blob was the number one requested Christmas gift for *parents* this year as well. They apparently use it to disgust their bosses."

"Well, the North Pole will not be delivering it!" Santa said. "I have Whimsy Elves who create fantastic gifts. I will not deliver BLOBS as presents!"

"I don't want a Blob," Kat whispered, hugging Antlers.

A sudden silence settled over the Toy Warehouse.

"What did you say?" Scoogie squinted at Kat.

Kat put her head down. "I said that I don't want a Blob. I'd rather play with my stuffed animal than some lousy little booger."

Santa, Mrs. Claus, and the Whimsy Elves smiled with delight.

Scoogie rolled his eyes. "And what about you, little boy?" He looked at Jackson.

"I'll be honest, sir; I've always wanted one." Jackson hesitated. "But I'm not sure playing with a Blob would be as fun as playing with my boomerang."

The other children nodded in agreement.

Santa chuckled with satisfaction. "Well then, it's settled! The North Pole will NOT be manufacturing Blobs. If we can teach the children in The School of Christmas Spirit the true meaning of playtime, we can teach the world."

"Good luck," Scoogie said sarcastically. "Though I have a feeling that we'll be getting a lot of returned rubber duckies."

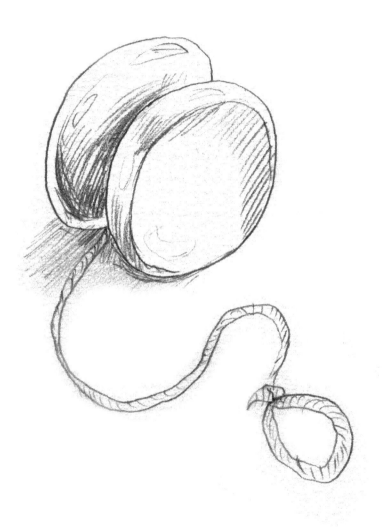

CHAPTER 7

Kat knew that she would have to select her final project topic before dinner that evening. Mrs. Claus had announced earlier in the day that during supper each student would be assigned a mentor; the mentor would be selected using a lottery system. At that time, the students would share their final project proposals with their mentors.

Kat already had a topic in mind. Ever since arriving in the North Pole, she had been mesmerized by the reindeer. On the way back to her dorm each evening, she purposely went out of her way to pass the stables and peek in at Blitzen, Dasher, and the rest of the gang. As an animal lover, Kat wanted to study the reindeer's innate wisdom. She wondered how they always knew where in the world to go, especially when she herself always felt like she was in the wrong place at the wrong time.

After a meal of peppermint mashed potatoes and gumdrop gravy, Mrs. Claus rang a fork on a glass in the dining hall to get the students' attention. Kat was so excited about the lottery that she accidentally knocked her tray onto her lap while clapping for Mrs. Claus. Gumdrop gravy splashed across her jumpsuit.

"Children, it's lottery time," Mrs. Claus announced. She held up a cone-shaped hat. "In this hat, we have the names of forty Elves that have passed their teaching certification course. They are ready and willing to mentor you through your final project."

Forty Elves lined up in front of the dining hall. Some, like Chip, Scoogie, and Mr. Nickel, were familiar to Kat. Others she'd never seen before.

"I hope I get Chip," Jillian whispered to Kat. "He seems like the most forgiving, and I want to do a project about his candyfruit garden."

Mrs. Claus read the names of the children alphabetically as she picked papers from the hat one by one. Jackson was paired with Zippy, who served as chief mechanic for Santa's workshop. Jackson high-fived his mentor, excited to work with him.

Jillian got Chip. She squealed with glee and ran to give him a hug.

Finally, it was Kat's turn.

"Kat McGee will be paired with…" Mrs. Claus paused for a dramatic moment. "Scoogie!"

Kat, still stained with gumdrop gravy, ran over to Scoogie. He reluctantly hugged her, careful not to touch her gravy stains.

"Hopefully you're not as sloppy with your paper as you are at the table, Kat McGee," he said with a smile.

"I'll be neat as a housemaid," Kat quipped. She imagined that Scoogie would be a mentor with high expectations. But she was excited to be working with Santa's cousin.

Later that evening, all the mentors were required to meet for an hour with their students to discuss their projects. Scoogie brought Kat to his office, which was cluttered with all sorts of gizmos and gadgets. Kat sat near his desk. Scoogie crossed his hands on one knee and looked her in the eye.

"So, Kat, what is your final project?"

Kat smiled. "I want to study the innate wisdom of the reindeer."

Scoogie laughed quietly. "The reindeer? You are the three hundredth student I've mentored with that idea. Oprah Winfrey, Kate Middleton, and Taylor Swift all did the same project."

"Well, the reindeer are pretty cool," Kat said.

"They're also boring," Scoogie said. "And next in line to be replaced," he added under his breath. "But if that's what you want to do…"

"It is!" Kat exclaimed.

Scoogie opened a drawer in his desk and pulled out a key. He handed it to Kat. "Here's the key to the stables. Do whatever you want, but make sure that you write the best paper in your class. Every student I've ever mentored has won the Class Prize for Best Independent Project. And I expect that this year will be the same."

"It will," Kat said with a nod.

"And don't forget that your paper is due at midnight on Christmas Eve. That only gives you two days, and time is ticking!"

The next day, Kat arrived at the stables at 6 AM and let herself in with the key. The reindeer were just waking, and seemed excited to see Kat.

Kat took a candyfruit from a nearby barrel, and fed it to Cupid. He nudged his nose against her hand in a loving manner.

"You're welcome," Kat said, smiling at the reindeer. She somehow knew that this was going to be one of the most rewarding projects of her life.

CHAPTER 8

Kat spent the rest of the day documenting the ways in which the reindeer communicated. She carefully studied their reactions to one another AND their reactions to Kat herself. The reindeer seemed open and comfortable with Kat, as if the girl was an old friend.

At the end of the afternoon, Kat jotted down her thoughts. Her notes were detailed and insightful. For example:

A. Prancer's antlers are ten inches longer than the other reindeer's antlers. Sometimes Prancer seems embarrassed by his long antlers, and he always keeps his head low to the ground.

B. Dasher stands facing south in the evening, and north in the morning. He keeps a list of numbers in his stall, with clear coordinates of latitudes and longitudes, so that he can understand locations around the world. Clearly, his innate sense of direction helps him lead the pack during the great Christmas delivery.

55

C. Donner and Blitzen, the most athletic of the reindeer, take an extra lap during each playtime in the field. They know that they need to keep up their stamina to provide extra oomph and help guide the back of Santa's sleigh.

After contemplating her many pages of notes, Kat realized that each of Santa's reindeer was unique in his own way. Their differences and strengths, Kat thought, made the entire pack stronger. It was exciting to realize that the seemingly similar reindeer were really individuals.

At sunset, as Kat was feeding the reindeer their dinner of apples and candyfruit, Jillian barged through the stable doors.

"Kat, Kat! Come quick! Mrs. Claus is holding an emergency meeting in her office! We're all required to attend!"

"An emergency meeting?" Kat asked, dropping her bucket of apples. "What on earth could be the emergency?"

Kat and Jillian and their other classmates packed into Mrs. Claus's office, shoulder to shoulder like sardines in the tiny space. Mrs. Claus paced back and forth, holding a tissue in her hand and occasionally rubbing her eyes.

"Thank you for coming on such short notice. I know you're all working hard on your final projects, but it seems reasonable to share the news with you in person."

Jillian whispered to Kat. "She doesn't look so good."

Mrs. Claus continued to blot her eyes with a tissue. "I have good news and bad news. The good news is that you are all invited to Santa's Annual Christmas Kick-Off Party tomorrow, the Joy Jubilee."

"Hooray!" the children yelled.

"The bad news," Mrs. Claus sniffled, "is that you are the last group of students who will ever attend this annual party."

"What?" the children asked, confused.

"Scoogie has run our numbers, and it seems we're financially unstable. Apparently, we haven't received our typical alumni support this year, despite regular attempts at fundraising. Unless we make a drastic financial change, the increased cost will bankrupt the North Pole. The only solution is to sacrifice funds from another part of campus. So, as of sunrise on Christmas morning, The School of Christmas Spirit will be closed."

All of the children gasped in unison.

"But what about you?" Jillian blurted out. "You're the heart of this school!"

"Thank you, Jillian," Mrs. Claus said. "I'll be fine, I suppose. The Whimsy Elves said that they needed a volunteer toy tester in the workshop, so I'll keep busy. They've assigned me to the rubber ducks. I'll squeeze them all day and make sure they quack."

"Duck quacking?" Kat blurted out. "I'm sorry, Mrs. Claus, but you are so much more than a rubber duck tester."

"Toy testing is an important job, too. And I don't have much of a choice now, do I?" Mrs. Claus forced a smile. Her eyes were teary. "Anyway, it's even more important to me now that every single one of you graduates, so hurry back to your projects. With the Joy Jubilee starting at 3 PM tomorrow, you'll need to use your time wisely in order to get your papers finished by midnight on Christmas Eve!"

The students slowly and silently exited the room, one by one.

That evening, Kat could hardly concentrate on her studies. Although she was excited about her reindeer research paper, she was too overcome with sadness about the closing of The School of Christmas Spirit to concentrate. She spent most of her time in the library nibbling on her nails and twirling her hair as she tried to think of ways to help Mrs. Claus.

Unfortunately, even after a long night, she found herself void of ideas and incredibly behind on her paper. And when she woke up, Kat was groggy and crabby. Even Chip couldn't cheer her up with his morning candyfruit.

Kat's rotten attitude seemed to be the norm across the North Pole. The kids in the library were sluggish and depressed. Even Jillian, who was typically as perky as caffeine, couldn't manage a smile.

"I don't understand," she said to Kat across a library table. "The School of Christmas Spirit has been around for decades. It doesn't seem right to close it now! There has to be a way to raise money to save it."

Kat's eyes opened wide. "Maybe we could have a lemonade stand fundraiser. Or a fashion show for charity! Or a candyfruit cookie bake sale."

Jillian frowned. "Mrs. Claus told Jackson that they need to raise over $100,000 …" She paused dramatically. "Per year."

Kat put her head in her hands, defeated.

At 2:45 PM, Kat and Jillian packed up their notebooks, and scurried to the courtyard for the Joy Jubilee.

The entire courtyard was brilliantly decorated. The central Christmas tree twinkled with white lights, and its boughs were decorated with gold tinsel. Ruby red holly and evergreen wreaths hung from each streetlight; Santa's sleigh runway, adjacent to the courtyard, was striped with a peppermint carpet.

On the perimeter, various booths were set up to entertain the crowd. One advertised, "Candy Apple Bobbing." Another invited hungry onlookers to try peppermint chocolate-chip ice cream. Still another booth challenged participants to "Reindeer Games," in which the students could throw hoops on Prancer's antlers.

Santa and Mrs. Claus sat at a table in the front of the courtyard. To their left, an Elf quartet played traditional Christmas carols. To their right, a juggling Elf kept a dozen candy canes in the air.

Although the entire North Pole was illuminated, Kat still felt dismal. Even with all the jubilee excitement, a feeling of loss filled the courtyard. Both the students and the Elves seemed a little less than celebratory.

When the North Pole clock tower struck 3 PM, Santa and Mrs. Claus rose from their seats. The Elves and students circled around them in respect.

Scoogie handed Mrs. Claus a microphone as she gave the benediction.

"Welcome one, welcome all, to the annual Joy Jubilee," Mrs. Claus said. A few pathetic claps echoed through the courtyard. Mrs. Claus scrunched her forehead.

"I said … Welcome to the annual Joy Jubilee!"

Still, only a few claps.

Mrs. Claus became angry. "Now, folks, don't be glum! Today is the most important day of the year, and I'm not going to let the closing of The School of Christmas Spirit ruin it. So, I'll say it ONE MORE TIME. Welcome to the annual Joy Jubilee!!"

The students and Elves clapped loudly, if only in support of Mrs. Claus.

"As always, the Jubilee will begin with the lighting of the official Christmas Tree. Every year, Santa and I choose one student from The School of Christmas Spirit who has impressed us with his or her commitment to service, kindness and overall humanity. I'm proud to announce that this year's tree lighter is … Jackson."

Jackson turned bright red as he walked to the front of the courtyard to meet Mrs. Claus. The students cheered.

"Congratulations, young man," Mrs. Claus smiled and motioned toward a nearby switch. "Go ahead. Turn it on."

Jackson flipped the switch. In a rush of light, the Christmas tree sparked to life, glowing like a star. Kat had never seen anything so beautiful.

"Wonderful," Mrs. Claus said. She turned to the nearby Baking Elves. "Bring out the cocoa!"

The Baking Elves carried out cups of hot cocoa for everyone in the courtyard. Giant marshmallows topped the liquid, oozing over the sides of the cups. In an instant, Kat's fingers were covered in marshmallow stickiness.

Mrs. Claus held her cup up in a toast. "Ladies and gentleman, students and Elves, cheers to…."

Santa interrupted. "Actually, Sadie, I'd like to give the toast this evening, if you don't mind. I have a little surprise for you. "

Mrs. Claus gave her husband a questioning smile, and stepped aside. Santa cleared his throat.

"Every year, we toast to health, happiness, and a holly jolly Christmas for all. But, this year, I want to add a special toast for the heart of our community, Mrs. Claus."

Kat whistled loudly as the other children cheered.

"Not only has my wife run The School of Christmas Spirit for the past seventy years, but she's also served as a loving grandmother to all in the North Pole. Although we are very sad about the closing of the School, we want to celebrate everything Mrs. Claus has achieved. We have specially designed an oversize commemorative snow globe, filled with miniature images of every graduate of The School of Christmas Spirit.

Tomorrow morning, this year's graduates will be included in the snow globe, and it will forever swirl with snow, to remind us of the scholars who once studied at this fine institution."

The students turned to marvel at the larger-than-life snow globe, which was unveiled with a flourish in the middle of the courtyard. The globe was beautiful, with the entire School of Spirit campus encapsulated in its glass walls.

"Now, lift your cocoa and toast the wonderful Mrs. Sadie Claus and The School of Christmas Spirit!"

"Hear, hear!" The Elves and children hollered, clinking their mugs and sipping their cocoa.

Mrs. Claus wiped a tear from her eye. Her husband gave her a kiss on her cheek.

"Well, aren't you going to ring it?" he asked, handing her the rope attached to the bell.

Mrs. Claus rang the bell. A beautiful note echoed throughout the North Pole.

"Now," Santa said, "I only have a few more hours until my sleigh takes off, so please go enjoy the Jubil…"

"NOT SO FAST," boomed a voice from the crowd. Scoogie stepped forward and took the microphone from Santa.

"You're not the only one with a surprise this evening," Scoogie smirked. "I have a surprise for Santa. And I have to say, mine is better than some silly snow globe."

Mrs. Claus and Santa raised their eyebrows, surprised.

Scoogie continued. "For those of you who don't know, tonight will be Santa's four hundred and fiftieth Christmas Eve delivery."

The students and Mrs. Claus clapped.

"On such an auspicious anniversary, I thought it appropriate to gift Santa with something to mark the next chapter in his already glorious career." Scoogie motioned to Chip, who stood near the back of the hall. Chip nodded and disappeared behind the hall doors. He re-emerged, pushing a sleigh on wheels.

"I would like to present Santa's new sleigh for this evening's delivery, the Red Sled 450-FX."

The students and Elves *oohed* and *aahed*. Santa looked utterly confused.

"The 450-FX is a specially-engineered, high-performance customized sleigh," Scoogie said, continuing his monologue. "Manufactured in Italy, it can reach speeds of two hundred miles per hour, and it has the ability to self-park."

"Self-park?" Santa asked, raising an eyebrow.

"Most importantly," Scoogie said, "it comes with a state-of-the-art GPS navigational system." Scoogie handed a small black device to Santa. "Instead of holding reins, you can hold this tiny GPS, and it will drive your sleigh for you! You could even take a nap, if you're feeling old and tired, and the sleigh will get you exactly where you need to be. Easy as candyfruit pie."

"I don't know about this," Santa said nervously.

"There's nothing to know," Scoogie smiled. "That's the beauty of it. Plus, I already had the Elves pack all of your presents in the trunk. It's ready to leave in ten minutes."

Without thinking, Kat stood up from her table. "But what about the reindeer?"

Scoogie looked at Kat. His smile reminded her of sharks she'd seen on the Discovery Channel.

"They'll be sent to the Bronx Zoo in New York. Where they'll be a hit, I'm sure."

Mrs. Claus put her hand on her husband's shoulder. "Scoogie, this is a very thoughtful gift. But I'm not sure that tonight is the right…"

"But Mrs. Claus, everything has been arranged! And Santa doesn't believe in returned gifts, now, does he?"

Santa stood and looked Scoogie in the eye. "No, I do not."

"And you're not too old to handle a little new technology, right?"

Santa took a deep breath. "I can handle anything," he said, glaring into Scoogie's eyes.

Mrs. Claus turned to her husband and whispered, "Are you sure about this, Nick?"

Santa nodded. "I can handle it, Sadie."

As the words came out of Santa's mouth, Kat felt worry begin to creep through her. She knew that Santa was capable, but she also knew that this would be his first journey without his trained reindeer. Thanks to her research, Kat knew how critical the reindeer had always been to his success.

Ten minutes later, Santa sat atop the Red Sled 450-FX, which was parked at the foot of the runway. His old sleigh sat deserted next to the garage. It was hidden in the shadows of the spotlight focused on the new Red Sled.

The Elves, students, and Mrs. Claus formed a semicircle around Santa. Moving to the very end, so she could be close to the action, Kat found herself next to Scoogie, who was snobbishly polishing the sleigh with a handkerchief.

At one point, Kat purposely sneezed on the sleigh, just to annoy Scoogie. He glared at her as he wiped away the germs.

Mrs. Claus held the official watch of the North Pole tight in her hand. She counted down the minutes until Santa's 8 PM lift-off.

"One minute, boys and girls."

"Now, how do you work this thing?" Santa asked Scoogie, gesturing toward the GPS.

"It's simple. All you need to do is enter the passcode and hold on. It will put you on the correct course."

"And what's the passcode?"

"Ten seconds," Mrs. Claus yelled.

"It's a series of numbers and letters. 90S00W." Scoogie was whispering, but Kat could still hear him. She had well-developed eavesdropping skills from listening to her brothers and sisters back home.

"Three ... Two ... One!" Mrs. Claus yelled.

Santa entered the code into the GPS. "90S00W," he muttered as he typed each letter.

"Blast-off!" Mrs. Claus announced.

The Red Sled shook, sputtered, and jetted down the runway at record-breaking speeds.

"Ho-Ho-Holy Moly!" Santa's voice trailed off as the sled disappeared from sight.

After Santa's departure, the North Pole fell still. A silent peace moved across the land as the Elves packed up the booths from the Jubilee and the students returned to the library.

Kat knew that she had less than four hours to finish her paper. She certainly wanted her named carved on the new commemorative bench, and she didn't want to disappoint Mrs. Claus. There was no time to waste.

But on her walk to the library, she realized that she still had the key to the reindeer stable in her pocket. Since Scoogie's office was on the way, she figured she would stop by and return it.

To her surprise, the light was on, but Scoogie was nowhere in sight. Kat shrugged, and looked around his office for a safe space to leave the key. It was cold and drafty; she sneezed loudly and tried to grab a tissue from the box on his desk.

But there were no tissues inside. Instead, Kat's fingers closed around a thin, rectangular piece of paper.

Pulling it out, Kat saw that it was a check for five thousand dollars from Kate Middleton. The subject line read, "For the education of future princesses at my alma mater".

Kat gasped and pushed the check back into the tissue box. As she did so, her hand brushed against what had to be other checks – tons of them! – stuffed in the bottom of the box. *How much money could possibly be in there?* Kat wondered.

The box of money reminded Kat of Mr. Mudge's envelope back in Totsville. She remembered her sisters warning her to keep quiet, how they'd told her nobody would believe her story.

She needed to leave the office immediately, Kat decided, before she got caught meddling in Scoogie's business. She sprinted towards the door—and at that moment, Scoogie entered. He jumped back in surprise.

"What are you doing in my office?"

"Nothing," Kat responded. "I mean … something. I mean, nothing! I mean … I was just coming to ask you a question about my paper."

"Well?" Scoogie said. "What is it? I'm very busy."

"Umm … I … umm," Kat fumbled. "I was wondering if the paper needed to be single-spaced?"

Scoogie furrowed his brow. "Young lady, you have three and a half hours to finish your paper. From what I've heard, you've barely formulated a thesis to explain your data. You have more to worry about than the spacing."

Kat looked down at her feet. "I just want to make sure that it's perfect."

"Miss McGee, let me warn you now: I'm a very tough grader. There is no such thing as a perfect paper. In fact, at this rate, you'll probably fail, and that will prove that you're still a … loser." Scoogie's face twisted into a wicked smirk. "It won't be so different from your track record, right, Miss … What did they call you back in Totsville? Kat McPee?"

The awful nickname sent feelings of woe and insecurity coursing through her in a mighty rush. Kat had never seen this side of Scoogie. His meanness was shocking. Her eyes welled up with tears; she turned away from Scoogie and ran out of his office.

Outside, under the Christmas Eve sky, tears streamed down Kat's cheek. Time was ticking, and her paper was barely written. She didn't want to fail out of The School of Christmas Spirit, and she certainly didn't want to cause any trouble.

And yet, she didn't want Mrs. Claus' school to close because of embezzlement.

In the cold night air, Kat's tears seemed to freeze on her face. Brushing them away, she paused in the middle of campus and looked up at the North Star. *At this instant*, Kat thought, *I'm standing in one of the most beautiful places on Earth*. Surely that meant something?

She remembered Dasher's coordinate chart from his stables, which noted that the North Pole was exactly ninety degrees North, zero degrees West.

Wow. Even if Scoogie thought she was a loser, Kat McGee was still literally on top of the world.

But wait. Ninety degrees North, zero degrees West sounded familiar. In fact, 90N, 00W, sounded similar to the number that Scoogie had set as a passcode for the Red Sled: 90S, 00W.

It couldn't be a coincidence.

At that moment, Kat knew what she had to do. Although her sisters hadn't believed her story back in Totsville, she knew that Mrs. Claus would believe her now. The School of Spirit had given her the confidence to believe in herself. And Kat knew that she must speak up to save Santa.

Kat ran directly to Mrs. Claus' house. The old lady was sitting in bed, reading *The Night Before Christmas* by candlelight. Kat barged in without knocking. She always forgot to knock, especially if it was important.

"Young lady!" Mrs. Claus sat up, shocked. "Where are your manners?"

"I'm so sorry to interrupt, ma'am. But this is really important."

"Why aren't you in the library? Your paper is due in just a few hours!"

"This is more important than my paper, Mrs. Claus. Scoogie has been hiding money from you and Santa. I think he's embezzling your alumni funds."

Mrs. Claus put her book down. "That's a very serious accusation, young lady. Do you have proof?"

Kat told Mrs. Claus about the checks in the tissue box. She spilled the beans about Kate Middleton's donation, and the fact that the box seemed to be filled to the brim with other money.

"But …Scoogie would never steal from us," Mrs. Claus stuttered. "We're family. Why, he's next in line to take over the North Pole if anything ever happened to Santa …"

"That's the problem!" Kat cried. "We need to save Santa. The passcode Scoogie gave him wasn't real! It was the coordinates for the South Pole. The Red Sled is taking Santa directly to the … the S Word! We have to save him!"

"The South Pole!" Mrs. Claus screamed. "No! Nobody is sending my Nicholas back to the South Pole without a fight from Sadie Claus!"

"Then, follow me! We need to get to the stables!"

CHAPTER 9

Kat used the key that she had yet to return to Scoogie to open the stable doors. The reindeer were lying down, depressed. Even Vixen, the most upbeat of the reindeer, wouldn't lift his head to greet Kat when she arrived.

"Dasher, Dancer, Vixen, get up!" Kat shouted as she barged in. Mrs. Claus followed, shaking her head.

"I'm not sure this is going to work," she said.

"Trust me," Kat said, grabbing Dasher's reins. "These reindeer are far more reliable than any stupid GPS. Help me get them outside to the old sleigh!"

Kat and Mrs. Claus led the reindeer out, one by one, and hitched them up. The reindeer had pep in their step as they took their regular posts. Kat could tell that they were excited to be needed in the North Pole once again.

"Don't forget their jingle bells." Mrs. Claus ran back into the stable and returned with eight jingle bells. She attached one to the breast collar of each reindeer. "For good luck."

As Kat and Mrs. Claus hustled to prepare the sleigh, a shadow appeared in the near distance. As it drew closer, Kat's eyes widened with fear.

"Hello, ladies," Scoogie said in a low, creepy voice. "Going somewhere?"

"You … you … scoundrel!" Mrs. Claus yelled. "You're Santa's cousin! How could you ruin the North Pole?"

"He ruined my childhood!" Scoogie shouted. "When he left the S Word and moved in with my family, all my parents ever cared about was him. I was always in his shadow, waiting for my turn in the spotlight. It's my time now!"

"Please don't hurt us," Kat begged.

"I won't hurt you," Scoogie smirked. "I'm just going to give you a new home. I have a nice spacious ice cave for you. But watch out … it's VERY chilly."

As he spoke, Scoogie pulled out a net and strode toward Kat and Mrs. Claus. They trembled with fear as he approached. His wicked scowl proved that he was certainly up to no good.

Suddenly, a pail swung out of the darkness and knocked Scoogie hard on the head. Kat's eyes widened with relief as Scoogie sank to the ground, unconscious. An instant later, a person popped out of the shadows, holding the pail. It was Jillian!

"I heard jingle bells in the stables and came to check on the reindeer," Jillian said. "Is everything okay?"

Mrs. Claus gave Jillian a hug. "It is now. Thank you, Jillian."

Kat smiled at her friend. "Thanks, Jill. But we need to run. There's too much to explain—we'll tell you everything when we get back! In the meantime, don't let Scoogie out of your sight."

Jillian snatched up a nearby rope and looped it around Scoogie's wrists. She tied it tightly and knotted the other end to the paddock gate. "Don't worry. He's not going anywhere."

Kat and Mrs. Claus climbed into the sleigh. Kat picked up the reins and shook them gently. "Okay, boys," she called. "Let's get this party started."

Dasher huffed; Dancer puffed. Comet and Cupid gave each other an antler bump of camaraderie. Prancer and Vixen kicked up their hooves. Donner and Blitzen stretched their legs.

"I hope you know what you're doing," Mrs. Claus said.

Kat concentrated hard. "On three. One, two … threeeeeeeeee!"

The reindeer moved in unison, galloping forward as the old sled tilted and rocked. Finally, Dasher and Dancer's feet hit the air, and the sleigh lifted into the sky, propelled by the reindeer's motion.

Jillian waved from the ground. "Be careful, Kat! See you soon!"

"Buckle your seatbelt, Mrs. Claus!" Kat cried. "It's going to be a bumpy ride!"

CHAPTER 10

After a few minutes in Santa's old sleigh, Kat grew more confident in her role as driver. This was much more exciting than the Rocket Roller Coaster at the Totsville Carnival, she thought as the sleigh soared through the air. She was enjoying being so high up … and she hadn't peed her pants.

Kat drove the sleigh with skill and direction. From her careful note-taking, she knew the reindeer's personalities and was able to lead them as a team, addressing each one individually, "Dasher, keep us headed due south! Cupid, you set the pace for the rest of the group."

Mrs. Claus gripped Kat's arm, eyes wide with anxiety. "We've got to find my husband. I can't imagine Santa being banished to *the S Word*."

"Keep your eyes on the sky!" Kat said. "Dasher is following his instincts south. With some luck, we'll be able to spot Santa before he's in real trouble!"

"There he is!" Mrs. Claus exclaimed, pointing into the distance. "There's the Red Sled 450-FX!"

Kat held tightly to the reins as the reindeer speeded up to a gallop. As they drew near, they saw Santa waving his hands in despair.

"Help me!" Santa yelled. "This sled won't stop! It keeps getting faster!"

Santa's sleigh curved and twirled in the night sky. Kat tried desperately to follow it.

"We're here to save you!" Kat called to Santa. "Just hold on!"

"I'm trying," Santa screamed, clutching the sled tightly.

"Mrs. Claus," Kat shouted, "I need you to hold the reins while I concentrate on coaching the reindeer."

Kat handed the reins to Mrs. Claus, who grabbed them with some hesitation. Taking a deep breath, Kat stepped to the front of the sled and wiggled toward Donner and Blitzen.

"Now, Donner! Now, Blitzen!" She started. "You've waited your entire lives for this moment. This is for every extra lap you've run in the yard. And every extra sprint before breakfast. You've been training hard, and this is your moment!"

Donner and Blitzen looked at Kat and let out a neigh.

"That's right, boys! Now, on three, push as hard as you can. It's your Olympics, and you're going for the gold." Kat patted the reindeer on the back. "I know you've got it in you. On three. One … two … THREE!"

Donner and Blitzen began to sprint at turbo speed. The sled sped into the sky and quickly caught up to Santa.

"Ho ho ho!" Santa exclaimed. "I knew those boys were special."

"You're doing great, guys! Keep up the pace!" Kat yelled to the reindeer. "We've got to stay right next to Santa. We'll be able to get him on the sled if we can just keep up!"

"But what about all the toys?!" Santa exclaimed, looking desperately at his oversized bag of presents. "They need to be delivered tonight!"

"Forget about the toys!" Mrs. Claus yelled. "The most important thing on that sled is YOU!"

"I'm not leaving without these toys!" Santa insisted. "I've never missed a Christmas, and I'm not going to let one bad sled ruin me now!" He hefted the massive bag in his arms, face full of determination. "Ready? Catch!"

Santa's aim was true: the bag of toys landed on the sleigh next to Mrs. Claus. But without the extra weight, the Red Sled immediately sped up.

"Nicholas! Hold on!" Mrs. Claus screamed. "You're going too fast!"

Kat looked around wildly, desperate for a way to get Santa off his runaway sleigh.

"We have to hurry!" Mrs. Claus said. "I'm not sure Donner and Blitzen are going to be able to keep up this speed!"

As she nodded, Kat's eyes fell on the other reindeer. "Prancer!" she exclaimed. She turned to Mrs. Claus. "Prancer can get Santa on the sleigh!"

Hearing his name, Prancer looked at Kat out of the corner of his eye.

"Prancer, boy, this is *your* moment. Your antlers. Your beautiful antlers. They're going to get Santa onboard!"

Prancer, who had always been embarrassed by his extra-long antlers, took a deep breath and slowly tilted his head toward Santa.

"You want me to hold onto Prancer's antlers?" Santa asked.

"Honey, it's that or be banished to the S Word!" Mrs. Claus yelled. "So buck up and grab hold of that reindeer!"

Prancer continued to tilt his head to the side as Santa grabbed his extended antlers. "WHOA!" Santa screamed, struggling to balance. After a wobble back and forth, he finally became secure on Prancer's back.

"Hooray!" Kat and Mrs. Claus cheered.

Santa patted Prancer, and the reindeer began to blush. "You *are* a special reindeer," Santa said. He looked around, smiling at all his hoofed friends. "You are ALL special reindeer!"

As Santa wiggled back to the sleigh, the Red Sled 450FX sped off into the distance. To Kat, Mrs. Claus, and Santa's horror, it erupted, exploding with a loud *poof* and sending a shower of sparks into the night sky.

"Oh, Sadie," Santa hugged his wife. "I'm so glad you're here."

"It's all because of Kat," Mrs. Claus said. "She saved you."

Santa turned to Kat and gave her a huge hug. "Not only did you save me, Kat McGee, you just saved Christmas! You're a real hero."

Kat had never considered herself a hero before. She blushed and handed the reins back to Santa.

"I think it's time to head home now," she said. "You can do the honors."

Santa shook his head. "We still have work to do." He looked back at the bag of toys and winked. "Care to join me on a Christmas Eve delivery mission?"

Kat nodded, heart skipping with excitement.

"Well, then, get us moving toward 9 Hummingbird Lane. Dorothy Jane was a good girl this year, and she definitely deserves a purple tricycle under her Christmas tree!"

"While Kat's driving," Mrs. Claus said to her husband. "I need to fill you in on some interesting happenings back at the North Pole."

CHAPTER 11

After an exciting night of Christmas Eve toy deliveries, Kat, Mrs. Claus, and Santa returned to the North Pole. The entire community of Elves and children stood, waiting on the runway. Cheers erupted as the reindeer landed safely, sleigh in tow.

Santa, however, had serious issues on his mind. Immediately, he approached the assembled Elves. "Where's Scoogie?"

"Over here!" Jillian yelled from the stable. Scoogie was conscious and back on his feet, but he was still tied tightly to the paddock.

"I didn't let him out of my sight," Jillian said, "but I did put some tape over his mouth. I was sick of hearing him talk."

Chip stepped forward. "Mrs. Claus, we did some further investigation while you were away, and found some interesting items in Scoogie's office."

One of the Baking Elves came up to stand beside Chip, and held up a piece of paper. "We found this – a letter to the sugar factory, ordering sour sugar for the candy canes."

One of the Whimsy Elves also stepped forward. "We found the actual list of "Most Wanted Christmas Toys" for this year, which lists The North Pole Rocking Horse as the most requested toy, not the Blob."

Mr. Nickel stepped forward. "And lastly, we found a box full of checks from various alumni of The School of Christmas Spirit."

Santa scratched his forehead. "I just heard about the checks. How much money was Scoogie hiding?"

"Well," Mr. Nickel said, "I ran some calculations. With the checks from alumni, we're still not financially stable."

The students were quiet, their disappointment hanging in the air.

"In fact," Mr. Nickel exclaimed, a huge smile breaking out on his face, "we're incredibly OVER budget. We have more than $100,000 in extra funds for The School of Christmas Spirit, in addition to the actual operating money!"

The students and Elves cheered blissfully. Amidst the sounds of celebration, Santa walked over to Scoogie and ripped the tape off his mouth.

"What do you have to say for yourself?" Santa asked in disgust.

Scoogie whimpered. "I … just wanted to be in charge."

"You'll be in charge, all right," Santa said. "From this day forward, you're in charge of picking up reindeer droppings. And you'll keep these ropes on your hands for a few months, long enough to re-earn the trust of the citizens of the North Pole."

"But Santa!" Scoogie exclaimed.

Santa took the tape and put it back over Scoogie's mouth.

"You're lucky you're my cousin. I'm only being this nice because you're family. For gosh sakes, Scoogie, you were the reason The School of Christmas Spirit almost closed!"

Mrs. Claus smiled, tears of joy shining in her eyes. "But it didn't! Effective immediately, I hereby pronounce The School of Christmas Spirit re-opened!"

Kat and her classmates cheered, jumping up and down with glee.

"And," Mrs. Claus continued, "I would like to announce this year's valedictorian. Let's hear it for Kat McGee!"

Kat's heart jumped—and then she remembered that she'd never completed her final assignment. "But Mrs. Claus, I didn't finish my report."

"Kat, you *used* the knowledge from your report for the greater good," Mrs. Claus said. "You truly embody the spirit of Christmas."

Jillian threw her arms around Kat and gave her a giant hug. As Kat's classmates erupted in cheers and whistles, she blushed. She couldn't believe it.

"As your valedictory gift, I present to you The School of Christmas Spirit Official Valedictory Snow Globe."

Kat took the snow globe from Mrs. Claus' hands. To her surprise, it looked exactly like the snow globe Gram had given her back in Totsville.

"Swirl it every Christmas Eve, and you can come back and visit," Mrs. Claus said. "We hope that you'll be our regular guest."

Kat smiled. "Definitely!"

All of the reindeer, Elves, and children circled around Kat as she held the snow globe. She gave it a swirl, and the snow inside began to fall.

Slowly, Kat grew drowsy. A few moments later, all of the Elves, children, and reindeer disappeared, fading away as her eyes drifted closed.

CHAPTER 12

It was Christmas morning at the McGee household. A light coat of snow covered the front and back yard, and the house twinkled with multi-colored lights. All of Kat's siblings had sprinted down the stairs towards the Christmas tree to admire the assortment of shiny, wrapped presents. The house was filled with the smell of Grandma's famous Christmas Day cinnamon rolls.

Kat slowly awoke from a deep slumber. She was back in her own bed, in her own room, in her own hometown. Gram sat next to her, brushing Kat's hair out of her face.

"Merry Christmas, my sweet little Kat. Sleep well?"

Kat blinked slowly. "I did, Gram. I slept incredibly well. In fact, I think I had a really weird dream."

"What was it?" Gram asked.

"Well, I was with your old friend, Sadie Claus. And she had a school. And I studied the reindeer. And I saved Santa. And …"

"Whoa, whoa, young lady," Gram smiled. "I think you'd better slow down and tell me the whole story. But first, I brought you up a tray of breakfast. I figured that you might enjoy a Christmas morning meal in bed."

Suddenly, a voice echoed from the hallway. It was Kat's little brother, Gus.

"GRAAMMM! Santa was here! Santa was here! Come quick!"

Grandma stood up and started walking towards the door. "I better go see your brothers and sisters," she said. "Don't tell the others about your surprise breakfast. It will be our little secret."

Kat reached for the covered tray of food, grabbing up a fork. To her delight, she lifted the lid and saw a small multicolored fruit sitting in the middle of the plate. Candyfruit! Kat took a bite, savoring the flavors of this North Pole delicacy. *Maybe it wasn't all a dream*, she thought.

Finishing the candyfruit, she hopped out of bed and ran downstairs to her family, who were gathered around the living room. The floor was covered with shredded wrapping paper and ripped ribbon. Gram and Kat's parents watched the Christmas morning revelry from the couch. Gus held tight to a brand new model airplane. Kat's sister, Polly, was playing with a North Pole rocking horse.

One present sat under the tree, still wrapped in shiny red paper and bound with white ribbon.

"I think that one's for you, Kat," Gram said.

Kat picked up the present. It was heavy, and the word "FRAGILE" was written in tiny penmanship on the top of the box. Kat remembered a lot of her siblings' presents from her time in the North Pole. But she didn't remember this one.

She slowly unwrapped the present, revealing the North Pole snow globe. The snow swirled madly inside it, even though Kat hadn't moved the globe.

"It's a magic snow globe," Kat said aloud.

"Magic?" Polly teased. "Nobody would ever believe that *you* had a magic snow globe."

Kat's siblings giggled, making Kat blush.

"It is magic," Kat said defensively. "I wouldn't lie."

"Give it to me, then!" Abe said, snatching the globe from Kat's hands. Immediately, the snow stopped twirling. Abe swished the globe around, but the snow stayed still.

"Let me hold it!" Kat's sister Hannah screamed, grabbing the globe. Still, the snow didn't move. "Stupid toy," Hannah said. "It's already broken." She shoved the snow globe back at Kat.

As Kat held it in her hands, the snow started to fall once more. Her siblings exchanged glances, marveling at her magic touch.

"You were telling the truth, Kat," Gus said. "Bring it over here, and let's play with it together."

"Yeah, Kat," Hannah said with a smile. "Come play with us!"

Kat and her siblings played with the snow globe for the rest of the day. Nobody could figure out why the snow only fell when Kat held the globe.

Nobody except Kat, of course.

And maybe her Gram McGee.

Rebecca Munsterer

Acknowledgments

Sometimes you just have to introduce yourself. Special thanks to Carey Albertine for inviting me to lunch after I introduced myself. This book would not have been written without the inspired vision of Carey and her In This Together Media partner, Saira Rao. I have tremendous respect for their courage, creativity, and craft. Also, I would like to thank Genevieve Gagne-Hawes for correcting my many grammar mistakes.

In addition, I would like to thank my mother for reading *The Night Before Christmas* by Clement Moore every Christmas Eve. All of the talk about reindeer certainly inspired this tale of the North Pole. I'm looking forward to providing my parents with a new Christmas story this year.

Lastly, I would like to thank Jamal, Molly, Jon, Gus, Emily, Wynne, and Mabel for encouraging my writing. My family and friends are the sugarplums of my life.

Kat McGee's Special Christmas Activities for Families

1. **To build *SELF-WORTH*:**

Imagine yourself in Santa's magic photo booth. You step in and a picture comes out that shows your biggest dream. Maybe you are walking on the moon? Maybe you are singing on a stage? Maybe you are working in the White House?

Now, dress up and have a friend take (or draw) a picture of your DREAM. Keep it on the bathroom mirror where you brush your teeth so you can see your dream every morning!

2. **To cultivate *WISDOM*:**

Make a naughty and nice list about YOU. Start with making a list of the NICE things. What things did you do this year that make you proud? When were you kind to others? How were you helpful to your family, friends, school, or community?

Next, make a naughty list. What are some of the NAUGHTY things you did? Were you unkind to someone? Were you disrespectful to your parents?

Now, put your list in a time capsule (shoe box) and store under your bed for the year. When you are feeling inspired, read the list of the NICE things you have done this past year. Forgive yourself for the NAUGHTY things, but vow to increase the length of your NICE list every year.

3. To encourage *WONDER*:

Invent the next big TOY or GAME for the Christmas season. What is it? How does it work? What does it look like? The Self-Propelling Swing Set? The Glow in The Dark Stuffed Animal? The Swimming Rubber Ducky? Draw an advertisement for this toy and share it with your friends.

4. To delight in *WHIMSY*:

Experiment in the kitchen and bake a new delicious Christmas cookie! Use sprinkles, chocolate chips, candy, or even gumdrops! Maybe you'll invent the Peanut Butter-Chocolate Surprise Cookie or a Marshmallow Mint Morsel Cookie? Write a recipe for your cookie and share a batch with a friend. The more creative, the better!

Remember to always ask your parents for permission to use the kitchen.

For ideas, see our special Candyfruit recipe on the next page!

From the Candyfruit Confectionary

The recipe for *Candyfruit* comes to you from the kitchens of Mah-Ze-Dahr Bakery. Pure ingredients mixed together in thoughtful and creative ways, this New York City-based bakery transports the curious on a delectable journey of mystery & desire. www.mahzedahrbakery.com

Yield: approximately 3/4 pound of candied fruit

> 3 large oranges
> 4 cups water
> 4 cups granulated sugar + 1 cup granulated sugar for coating the peel
> 4 ounces dark chocolate, chopped into small pieces (or you can use dark chocolate chips)

Rinse oranges under cold water, then wipe them dry. Cut about a quarter-inch off each end of the orange. With a sharp paring knife, cut through the peel and into the white pith. Slice through the peel from the top of the orange to the bottom. Cut almost all the way through the pith but stop before you get to the fruit. Make that same cut about a quarter of the way around the fruit, making a total of four cuts into the orange. Cut a shallow cut into the top of the orange at the edge of the peel, all the way around the orange. These cuts are meant to create sections that you can peel off easily. Wiggle your finger between the orange and the peel. Work your finger down under the peel to separate the peel from the fruit. Once you've removed the whole peel section, repeat the finger wiggle thing on all the other peel sections. Do the same with the other oranges. Slice each piece of orange into thin strips, each a little less than a centimeter wide.

Now, blanch the orange peels. This is done to take the bitterness out of the pith. Boil a few inches of water in a medium-sized pot over high heat. Once the water is boiling, drop in all the sliced orange peels. Stir the slices to soak them in the water. Boil for 20 minutes. Drain the peel pieces in a colander. Run under cold water until the peels are cool to the touch, for about a minute.

Now simmer the peel pieces in the sugar syrup. Put 4 cups water and 4 cups sugar in a medium-sized, heavy-bottomed pot. Whisk to combine. Over high heat, bring the syrup up to a boil. Whisk occasionally until all the sugar melts. Once the sugar syrup is boiling, carefully add the balanced peels to the pot. Be very careful when adding in the peel pieces so as to not get burned. Stir the peels a bit. Maintain a rolling boil (lower the heat a little) and boil the peels for 45 minutes. Keep checking the pot, especially after 30 minutes, to ensure the pot doesn't boil over. When the peels are done, they will be translucent and look clear and jellied.

Now drain and dry the orange peels. Take a baking sheet and lay paper towel on it. Then place a cooling rack on top of the paper towel-lined baking sheet. This will catch all the dripping syrup. Using a fork, take out a few pieces of peel at a time. Set the pieces on the prepared rack to drain. Repeat until all the peel pieces are on the rack. Separate the pieces out so they're not touching. Let the peels drip dry for about 15 minutes.

Now decide if you want to dip the pieces in chocolate or roll in sugar. For all the pieces you want to eat without chocolate, you will roll them in sugar. Separate out the pieces you want to dip in chocolate. For the others, put 1 cup of sugar in a medium-sized bowl. Drop a few pieces of the peel into the sugar.

Roll the pieces around to coat them all over. Shake off the excess sugar and place on a clean cooling rack set on top of a baking sheet covered in paper towel (don't put them back on the original rack because that one is already full of sticky syrup!). Repeat this process with the rest of the peels you're not dipping in chocolate. Space them out so they're not touching. Leave them uncovered overnight to dry out. If you just can't wait, place the sugar-coated peels on a parchment-lined baking sheet in a 200 degree oven for 15 minutes. That should dry them out faster.

If you want to dip the peel pieces in chocolate, melt the chocolate in a microwave-safe bowl at high power for 1 minute. Remove the bowl and stir the chocolate. If it's not fully melted, put the bowl back in the microwave and heat for an additional 30 seconds. Remove and stir until the chocolate is completely smooth. After the peels have dried for 15 minutes, take the peels one at a time, hold at one end and dip them into the melted chocolate. Leave about 1/4 to 1/2 of the peel naked, and cover the rest in chocolate. Place on a parchment-lined baking sheet to set and dry overnight.

Now don't forget, you have some delicious orange-flavored syrup. You can use it to flavor sparkling water, iced tea, and for the parents, some wonderful cocktails!

About Rebecca Munsterer

Rebecca Munsterer is the author and creator of Novel Nibble, an online website devoted to both serial fiction and musings about writing. An avid non-fiction writer as well, Rebecca has published articles in *SKI*, *ISLANDS*, *Reader's Digest*, and various other periodicals. During the day, Munsterer works as the Senior Associate Director of Admissions at Dartmouth College where she reads over two thousand college essays annually. Rebecca lives in Norwich, Vermont where she finds inspiration for characters among the townsfolk.

Connect with Rebecca:

Website: NovelNibble.com/
Twitter: @NovelNibble
Facebook: Facebook.com/NovelNibble

Other Books by
In This Together Media

Kat McGee and The Halloween Costume Caper by Kristin Riddick

Soccer Sisters: Lily Out of Bounds by Andrea Montalbano

Soccer Sisters: Vee Caught Offside by Andrea Montalbano

Playing Nice by Rebekah Crane

Personal Statement by Jason Odell Williams

Connect with us!

Website: www.inthistogethermedia.com/
Twitter: @intogethermedia
Facebook: facebook.com/InThisTogetherMedia
facebook.com/AKatMcgeeAdventure
Pinterest: Pinterest.com/ITTMedia

Reading Guide

Please enjoy this chapter-by-chapter reading guide, ready-made to engage your upper elementary school student in an interactive and social literacy experience. Students will expand their knowledge of this adventurous plot by examining vocabulary and character choices and will relate to the story on a personal level by answering reflective discussion questions. We've also included hands-on, collaborative, cross-curricular activities that will enhance your child's experience and understanding, all the while providing them with a world of fun! We hope you enjoy this resource. For more educational and character-building activities, visit <u>beanoblekid.org</u>.

CHAPTER 1

Vocabulary Words: companionship, reinvent, coveted, deliberation, bribe, devastation

Discussion Questions:

1. How did Kat get her unfortunate nickname?

_____

_____

_____

_____

Have you ever been given a nickname? _____

If so, what was it, and how did it make you feel?

_____

_____

_____

_____

2. Why did Kat feel that she was just average?

_____

_____

_____

_____

3. How did Kat plan to reinvent herself?

_____

_____

_____

_____

4. How do you think Kat felt when she wasn't chosen for the part of Mary?

_____

_____

_____

_____

5. Kat thinks the pageant was rigged. What do you think, and why?

_____

_____

_____

_____

6. Who taught Gram about the wonders of cinnamon?

_____

_____

_____

_____

Activities:

Create a family tree for Kat McGee. Include her grandparents, parents, brothers and sisters, and pets.

Kat McGee's Family Tree

Kat's brothers and sisters say and do some very hurtful things to her, when they could have supported their sister. Write a paragraph explaining why it is so important to support your siblings and closest friends, especially when they are going through difficult times. Give examples of how you can show your support.

Use the instructions below to make your very own, original snow globe.

YOU'LL NEED:

Small clean jar with a lid (baby food or condiment jars are good choices)

A piece of sandpaper

Small plastic figures or waterproof decorative objects that will fit in the jar

Hot glue gun or super glue

Distilled or bottled water

Glycerin (available at drug stores or craft stores)

Glitter

Colored electrical tape (optional)

1. Remove the lid from the jar and lightly sand the inside of the top.

2. Position figures on the lid.

3. Glue in place. Let dry.

4. Fill jar about 7/8 full with water. Add 3-4 drops of glycerin.

5. Add 2-3 teaspoons of glitter.

6. Close jar.

7. Glue closed or seal with electrical tape.

8. Lightly shake and smile.

CHAPTER 2

Vocabulary Words: fidgety, tousled, rehabilitate, disposition, distinguished, jealousy, greed, commence, reconvene

Discussion Questions:

1. When Kat awakes, who is there to greet her and where is she?

_____

_____

_____

_____

2. Who is Scoogie? _____

_____

_____

3. What are The Four Tenets of Spirit?

1. _____

2. _____

3. _____

4. _____

4. What do the children have to do in order to graduate from the School of Christmas Spirit?

_____

_____

_____

_____

Activities:

The School of Christmas Spirit educated some of the finest world leaders: Martin Luther King, Jr., Mother Theresa, and Barry Manilow. Research each of these leaders and list 5 things that they did to impact the world.

Martin Luther King, Jr.

_____

_____

_____

_____

_____

_____

_____

Mother Theresa

_____

_____

_____

_____

_____

_____

_____

_____

Barry Manilow

_____

_____

_____

_____

_____

_____

_____

_____

Draw a picture of the Earth, and illustrate what you think the North Pole and the "S" word look like, based on the information in this chapter. Include as many details as you can.

CHAPTER 3

Vocabulary List: warily, chortled, relentlessly, potential, malfunction, anecdotes, myriad, perplexed

Discussion Questions:

1. On the way to Nicholas Hall, Kat talked with her new friends Jackson and Jillian, who each envied something that she had. What did they envy, and why?

_____

_____

_____

_____

2. Why did Kat admire Mrs. Claus so much?

_____

_____

3. According to Mrs. Claus, what is the definition of **worthiness**?

_____

_____

_____

_____

4. What is The Photo Booth of Potential?

_____

_____

_____

_____

5. What did The Photo Booth of Potential tell Kat about her future?

_____

_____

_____

_____

Activities:

Create your own candyfruit. Combine your favorite fruit and your favorite candy and list the vitamins and benefits that it possesses, just as Chip did when he was serving Kat breakfast. Design your own packaging and present it to your class, or family.

Follow the recipe in the back of the book to bake the original candyfruit served to Kat in the North Pole.

CHAPTER 4

Vocabulary List: infirmary, distinguishing, gingerly, ostentatiously, relentless, intuition

Discussion Questions:

1. How do you think Kat felt when she pressed the "X" button for her own brother, Abe?

_____

_____

_____

_____

_____

_____

2. Why did Kat stand up to Mr. Nickel, and tell him that she didn't want to classify the boys and girls as "naughty" or "nice" anymore?

_____

_____

_____

_____

3. According to Mr. Nickel, why did Kat pass the Tenet of Wisdom?

_____

_____

_____

_____

4. Use context clues to write the definition for the word **wisdom**.

_____

_____

_____

_____

Activities:

Kat didn't think it was fair to label people based on a ten-second video, and stood up for what she believed in. Choose something that you have observed in your life (at home, at school, or elsewhere) that you don't think is fair. Write an argument for why it isn't fair, and create a new system, or approach, that would make it fair.

CHAPTER 5

Vocabulary List: emitted, permeated, stifle, intimidating, distinctly, savory, confirmation, disheartened

Discussion Questions:

1. According to Mrs. Claus, what does the word **wonder** mean?

_____

_____

_____

_____

2. What mistake led Gram to create one of her most delicious meals?

_____

_____

3. Do you think there is something wrong with Santa, and do you think he will be okay?

_____

_____

_____

_____

4. What do you predict will happen in the next chapter?

_____

_____

_____

_____

Activities:

Design your own Christmas cookie. Follow Mrs. Claus' instructions on page 48.

CHAPTER 6

Vocabulary List: diverse, magnitude, innovating, interjected

Discussion Questions:

1. What is inside building ABCD?

_____

_____

_____

_____

2. According to Mrs. Claus, what is the definition of the word **whimsy**?

_____

_____

3. The Whimsy Elf concluded his presentation by saying, "Now, boys and girls, always continue dreaming and exploring, creating and innovating. For the magic of toys is the magic of the imagination." What do you think this means?

_____

_____

_____

_____

4. Would you want to receive a Blob over a boomerang, or a stuffed animal? Why, or why not?

_____

_____

_____

_____

Activities:

Kat donated her leftover Salted Cinna-Water-Nana cookies to the "Save the North Pole Penguin" food bank. Research local charities, and choose one that you would like to donate to.

Choose a toy, or design your own, that reflects your unique personality. Present it to your class, or family, and explain why you chose that particular toy.

CHAPTER 7

Vocabulary List: mentor, innate, reluctantly

Discussion Questions:

1. What topic does Kat choose for her final project?

_____

_____

_____

_____

Activities:

Pretend that you are Kat. Do some research and on the lines below, write a paragraph about the innate wisdom of reindeer.

CHAPTER 8

Vocabulary List: insightful, stamina, drastic, adjacent, dismal, commemorative, encapsulated, auspicious, meddling, embezzlement, accusation

Discussion Questions:

1. What is the bad news that Mrs. Claus shares with all of the students?

_____

_____

_____

_____

2. Why was Jackson chosen to light the official Christmas Tree of the Joy Jubilee?

_____

_____

3. When Scoogie presents the new sled to Santa and explains what has been arranged, how does it make you feel about him?

_____

_____

_____

_____

4. When Kat went looking for tissues, what did she find instead?

_____

_____

_____

_____

5. When Kat figured out what the passcode for the Red Sled meant, she knew what she had to do. What gave her the confidence to be able to speak up?

_____

_____

_____

_____

6. Why do you think Scoogie would do all of the mean things that are discovered in Chapter 8?

_____

_____

_____

_____

Activities:

When studying the reindeer, Kat realized that each had unique strengths and differences that made the entire herd stronger. Study your family, record each family member's strengths and differences, and describe how these strengths and differences make your family stronger.

Host your own Joy Jubilee. Set up various game booths, play music, have a craft table, and serve baked goods and hot cocoa to your friends and family to celebrate the season.

Draw a picture of what you think the Red Sled 450-FX looks like.

CHAPTER 9 - CHAPTER 12

Vocabulary List: camaraderie, instincts, determination, banished, delicacy, revelry, defensively

Discussion Questions:

1. Prancer had always been embarrassed by his extra-long antlers. Have you ever been embarrassed by one of your physical traits? If so, what is it, and write down one reason it is a good trait to have.

2. What do you imagine it would be like if Santa asked you to join him on Christmas Eve to deliver all of the gifts to the good boys and girls?

_____

_____

_____

_____

_____

_____

_____

3. What surprise breakfast did Gram bring to Kat on Christmas morning?

_____

_____

_____

_____

What do you think this means?

_____

_____

_____

_____

4. What made the North Pole snow globe that Kat got for Christmas magic?

_____

_____

_____

_____

5. What do you think Kat learned about herself from her Christmas adventure in the North Pole?

_____

_____

_____

_____

Activities:

Complete **Kat McGee's Special Christmas Activities for Families** found in the back of the book.

For more educational and character-building activities, visit beanoblekid.org

24571028R00078

Made in the USA
Charleston, SC
27 November 2013